THE INTERLOPER

THE INTERLOPER

a novel

Antoine Wilson

HANDSEL BOOKS

an imprint of Other Press • New York

Production Editor: Mira S. Park
Text design: Natalya Balnova

This book was set in 11.5 pt ACaslon by Alpha Graphics of Pittsfield, NH.

10 9 8 7 6 5 4 3 2 1

Library of Congress Cataloging-in-Publication Data

Wilson, Antoine.
The interloper / Antoine Wilson.
    p. cm.
ISBN-13: 978-1-59051-263-0 (acid-free paper)
ISBN-10: 1-59051-263-4 (acid-free paper) 1. Murder victims'
families–Fiction. 2. Prisoners–Fiction. 3. Revenge–Fiction. I.
Title.
PS3623.I5778I67 2007
813'.54–dc22
                                        2006014546

To Chrissy

Acknowledgments

Thank you to Eric Bennett, Connie Brothers, Dana Goodyear, Brigid Hughes, Rosanna Levinson, Jack Livings, James Alan McPherson, Zoe Pagnamenta, Carol Houck Smith, John Woodward, and my parents. Also, for their generous support, the Wisconsin Institute for Creative Writing, where I was fortunate to spend a year as the Carol Houck Smith Fellow in Fiction Writing.

Passing stranger! you do not know how longingly I look upon
   you,
You must be he I was seeking, or she I was seeking, (it comes to
   me, as of a dream,)
I have somewhere surely lived a life of joy with you,
All is recall'd as we flit by each other, fluid, affectionate, chaste,
   matured,
You grew up with me, were a boy with me, or a girl with me,
I ate with you, and slept with you, your body has become not
   yours only nor left my body mine only,
You give me the pleasure of your eyes, face, flesh, as we pass,
   you take of my beard, breast, hands, in return,
I am not to speak to you, I am to think of you when I sit alone
   or wake at night alone,
I am to wait, I do not doubt I am to meet you again,
I am to see to it that I do not lose you.

—WALT WHITMAN, To a Stranger

The Interloper

1

My name is Owen Patterson. I am thirty-eight years old. I am in fine shape medically and psychologically. I have been checked out on both counts. Despite my being far away from her, and my not having talked to her for several months now, I remain married to Patricia Patterson, née Stocking. We have no children. I consider myself a civilized person, probably around 80% acclimated to the society in which I lived, if not more. A solid B. I miss working for the software company. Life had a nice routine to it. Software manuals are pleasingly logical when written right, and we used to write them right. If I could wake up from this bad dream, I would wake up in my cubicle at the software company, face creased from the edge of a binder, and ask mouth-breathing Neil, in the next cubicle over, if he wanted to get some coffee downstairs.

They won't give me access to any of my files or letters. This account is an escape hatch that opens into deep water. If the man who murdered Patty's brother had been executed for his crime, if our justice system had been just, we might have been able to move on, we might have continued in a state of normalcy, however fragile. But the soil of our marriage was poisoned. Not by her brother's murder. By the twenty-odd-year sentence handed down to the man who had taken CJ's life. Twenty years—three square meals a day, a warm place to rest, friends and associates of like criminal mind—for taking CJ away forever.

I was present at the sentencing. I was the stiff man in the blue suit on whose lapel the victim's sister quietly sobbed. Calvin Senior and I were two pillars of male strength, and we supported our weeping wives, as it was supposed to be. There was no admission of guilt from Henry Joseph Raven, no apology to the family, just a smile and a wink to a woman in the gallery as they led him away. He had no idea what he had done to the Stockings. He did not care, and the Stockings could see this, and there was no finality. The world was an unbalanced equation—you could write it down, it was there in front of you on paper, but it was fundamentally wrong.

Over a year after Henry Raven had been put away, Patty sat at the Stocking family dinner table with her parents, with me. She wore all black. There was no continuity between the Patty I'd married and the Patty whose brother had been murdered. The soil had been poisoned. We sleepwalked through our lives. She worked the night shift at the pharmaceutical company, I wrote software documentation, half at the office, half at home. We saw each other when we could. I once snuck out to Patty's work to surprise her. In the lab she wore a sterile suit, and I was desperate to see her in something that wasn't black. I couldn't get past security. If I had known how, I would have paid someone to kill Henry Raven in prison.

That night at dinner, I was optimistic for the first time in months. After a false start I will relate below, I had stumbled across a means by which Raven would suffer appropriately for his crime, a way to tip the scales, bring things back to normal, show the Stockings that justice had been done, that CJ's death had not been met with a wink and a smile, but with just punishment.

First, dinner. Every family comprises a little metaphysical universe, and the addition or subtraction of a member can throw off the balance completely. Despite the fact that the Stockings had lost CJ—he was murdered while Patty and I were on our honeymoon—they'd gained me. I sat in his seat, but I did not possess the same appetite he did. CJ was known for his ability to eat seconds and thirds at every meal. I am a slow eater, due to some scar tissue in my esophagus I have never had repaired; also, I could not stand Minerva's cooking. Everything was unsalted—for the benefit of Calvin Senior's heart—and the only salt on the table was potassium salt, which was not salt. Patty had grown up on bland food, and had attuned her taste buds to it, while I had grown up foraging in my aunt and uncle's kitchen (tortilla chips, corn dogs) and couldn't taste Minerva's flavorless cooking.

Calvin Stocking Senior was big and silent, bearish not in terms of hairiness but of his long and lumbering body, upon which had been placed a small head. At dinner, he still wore his tie from work, and the way the flesh of his thick neck bulged above his starched white collar reminded me of those dogs whose skulls are too small for their brains. Minerva Stocking was the rounder of the two, not fat so much as plump, and she could be depended upon to wear various mystical stones, crystals, turquoise and the like, to accentuate her suburban outfits. If she had not talked, dinner would have been quiet. She was a great believer in signs. She gave me a card not long after CJ's death that said "Everything Happens For A Reason—American Proverb." A number of highly successful people are deeply susceptible to signs, and I have come to believe that many of them use this technique in order to commune with their unconscious minds. I have tried it from time to time, but find that my ego, if there is such a thing, will not let go easily. Her permanent subject was her murdered son. Phrases like "CJ would have loved this" and "If only CJ were here to see this" poured out in a steady stream of talk. Calvin Senior joined her in the talk, never enthusiastic but also never reluctant.

It was not the custom of my family to speak of the dead for too long after they were gone. When my cousin Eileen died, we established a tacit agreement that after the mourning period had come to an end, we would no longer speak of her unduly. We did this out of consideration for each other, to put the mourning behind us. Or, more accurately, to keep it bottled within us, hidden away, to reappear only when someone spoke tactlessly and scraped the old wound, or in dreams. To bring her up was to risk rousing emotions. Patty's family was not afraid of emotions; theirs came out in Little Stocking Pieces instead of Frustrated Patterson Outbursts.

"Tonight we're having CJ's favorite," Minerva announced from the kitchen, "T-bone steak and new potatoes."

Even as I began to gain control over my physical responses to this talk about the dead, even as I felt like I was getting used to it, I shivered at every mention of CJ. They would never finish talking about him.

Minerva looked at me across the table and asked what I thought of the tahini dressing.

I smiled and said, "What goes into that, exactly? I might want to throw some together at home."

She listed ingredients and ran down some preparation instructions, which I forgot immediately. Patty knew what I was doing. She called it "baiting" her mother. She was highly attuned—possibly overattuned—to insincerity. Her mother suffered from no such sensitivity.

"Tell my parents how work is going," said Patty.

"We're doing a total revision of a manual for our accounting software. My boss wants to go head-to-head with the third-party manuals. I'm not sure why. It's a lot of writing."

"You know CJ used to write," Minerva said.

"He did not," Patty said.

"Now, now," said Calvin Senior, "let your mother speak."

"Writing was his favorite subject. We used to get all kinds of notes from his English teachers, talking about how creative his papers were. Now, they weren't always supposed to be creative, but leave it to CJ. He was irre—something—ible that way."

"Irresponsible?" I offered.

"Irrepressible," said Patty.

"Yes. That."

Typically, Minerva brought him up, Patty resisted, and Calvin Senior let it be known that they were going to talk about what Minerva wanted to talk about. After which Patty eased into CJ-talk herself.

I was a fresh audience, an opportunity to build CJ from the ground up. I had already begun hearing repeated stories. In some ways I was becoming one of them. Except I felt little sense of loss, vis-à-vis CJ. I had only met him in person a few times. Since I had gotten to know him through stories, I hadn't really lost anything. The stories kept coming.

The Stockings never talked about the murder. They found a way to bring CJ's memory into just about any conversation, but the murder itself was taboo. They never mentioned Henry Joseph Raven. He had become just another manifestation of a generalized evil force that existed "out there." They simply missed CJ, as if he had died in a car accident or scaffolding collapse. I suppose they had some ideas about vengeance corrupting the soul.

Here's what I pieced together from the newspapers and the trial: CJ had been drinking in a seedy restaurant-bar in the Rockies called Diana's Grill, not far from where he attended college. His girlfriend had broken up with him, and he'd gone to Diana's to drown his sorrows. The toilet had overflowed earlier in the evening, so when nature called, he went out back to relieve himself, as was the local custom. There, he encountered two men, Henry Joseph Raven and his accomplice, Hoden Broadbent Murray. The men abducted CJ from the dirt lot behind the bar and took him to his Chevy Blazer. They drove him to a remote location in the mountains, some seventy-five miles away. There, Henry Raven shot CJ in the back of the head and left his body in some trees by the side of the road. Murray, upon hearing the gunshot, panicked and fled the scene in the Blazer. He had the foresight to reset the trip odometer. If he hadn't, they might never have found CJ's body. That courtesy, along with his willingness to testify against Raven, earned him a lesser charge. Raven was apprehended a week later. His story, that the three men had been partying together all night, and that he had not been present when CJ was shot, was contradicted by several witnesses, prime among them his former accomplice, Murray. But Murray had struck a deal with the prosecutors, and had every reason to bend the story to his advantage. Prosecutors had to hang the case on forensics, matching the lead of the bullet found in CJ with the lead of bullets discovered at Raven's home. In the end, Raven's strategy of denial meant the difference between the death penalty and a twenty-some-year stint with the possibility of parole. In the library's newspaper database, I cross-referenced "Henry Joseph Raven" and "miscarriage of justice." My search returned fourteen hits, all opinion pages from Colorado and California newspapers.

Minerva stood over the serving dish. "Seconds?" she asked.

My plate was nowhere near clean; as a matter of fact, I was still cutting and chewing my dinner. "It's delicious," I said.

"I wondered if you want some more?"

I looked at my plate.

"Can I get back to you on that?"

Patty intervened. "He's still eating, Mom. They're not seconds if the firsts aren't done yet."

Minerva remained over the dish. "I just didn't want his plate to go empty." She gestured with a large two-pronged fork. "Besides, there's still a nice big piece of steak left. Someone's going to have to eat it."

Calvin Senior looked up. He had tolerated his wife's flavorless cooking since the doctor said he should cut down his salt intake, and he had never complained about it once. But he wasn't going to go as far as taking these leftovers to work.

"I've got lunch at the club tomorrow," he said.

"We're having a catered meeting," Patty said.

Minerva turned to me. What could I say? I was working at home the next day. I would either eat it now or then. "I'd be happy to take it home for lunch, if you're willing to wrap it up."

She frowned and turned toward the kitchen with the dish.

"Mom!" Patty looked at her sternly. "We're still eating."

I scanned the table. Calvin Senior had finished, as had Patty. Minerva's plate was empty save a bone and a few gristly bits. I was still eating. Not we. I.

"It's okay," I said.

"It is not okay," said Patty. "It is rude to get up from the table before everyone has finished."

"I'm almost there, anyway, and I'm a slow eater. Happens all the time."

"It's a matter of principle."

It was not a matter of principle, exactly. Patty could become stubborn, ornery, obtuse, and downright rude whenever coming to my defense. She would ignore a thousand flaming arrows shot in her direction, but if a pebble landed at my feet, she would cry foul. Her loyalty to me was a badge of pride, and as such, it didn't always conform to reality. It disturbed me that this one component of our love had survived while so many others had fallen by the wayside. This person, who in so many ways no longer resembled the woman I married—who wore nothing but black, who had switched to work the night shift, who rejected my clumsy attempts at intimacy—this person clung to the detritus of our early love the way a castaway clings to a waterlogged mast.

"We're not finished eating," Patty said.

Minerva sat down. She knew she could not win this battle. I ate as quickly as I could, which due to my medical condition was not exceedingly quick. I tried, between bites, while the food was making its way around the curves and bumps of my scarred esophagus, to keep the conversation going.

"What we need here," I said, "is CJ. He would have eaten up this stuff lickety-split."

They all stared at their plates. I expected some laughter, a jump-started anecdote.

"He would have though, right?" I asked. "I mean, the kid could eat."

"Please just finish," Patty said.

After dinner Calvin Senior and I ended up in the den while Patty and her mother occupied themselves in the kitchen. Normally the four of us would have stayed together in the kitchen or the den, but that night we had rented *Vertigo*, and the boys had been assigned the task of prepping the video machine while the girls put together desserts. Setting up the video took only a moment. In an attempt to find some common ground with Calvin Senior, I tried to talk sports with him, but I was never much of a sports person, and so I ended up feeling as if I were a boy picking up his daughter for a first date. Though he had begun to warm to me somewhat, calling me "son" now and then—with a wink I never understood—I always felt a gap between myself and this bear of a man. Patty and her mother thought of him as a large, docile, cuddly creature, but I saw the claws, and I saw that he was not afraid to display them to me at opportune moments. Life with his wife and daughter was a sort of act, an act he found pleasant to immerse himself in while also maintaining other acts for, say, the men at the club, or the secretaries at the office. The act he'd reserved for me had not really changed since I'd started dating Patty. There was something mildly distasteful in his getting chummy with the man who was intimate with his daughter and had such great potential to hurt her by turning out to be just another asshole. All men were assholes. The art of being a man was in acting like a gentleman and saving the frat boy crap for places like the club. I knew I could never replace Calvin Junior. Every time CJ was invoked, I felt that I was some sort of inadequate stand-in, a changeling, a pretender. My father-in-law did little to make this feeling go away.

The subject at the dinner table had been Calvin Junior, and now Calvin Senior seemed ready to continue it, albeit in a different key. He walked up to the mantle and picked up a picture. Images of CJ were interspersed among early Calvin and Minerva portraits, family vacation shots, and pictures of Patty blooming, awkwardly, in time-lapse. A shrine to CJ would have made me feel more comfortable. What they had up on the mantle did not acknowledge that CJ was gone at all. A burglar would have assumed that he was still a living, breathing member of the family. Over the years, of course, everyone would grow older but him.

Calvin Senior held up the picture, CJ on the beach with his surfboard, and said to me, as if to explain his thoughts in that moment of silence: "The guy who did this is in jail. When I think of what he did to my son, I think that prison rape is not such a bad thing." He put the picture back. "I'd kill him with my bare hands if I got the chance. But I won't get the chance. I don't want the chance, usually."

The door to the kitchen clunked and swung open—my wife and her mother, holding desserts. Calvin Senior looked at me and shook his head almost imperceptibly. I understood. Not a word to anyone, the dissenting opinion is sealed up in its envelope, now try to pretend we were talking about something else. But they would go on talking about CJ, Patty would go on wearing black, Calvin Senior would go on steaming quietly, grumbling inside . . . the body decays, the memories jumble, the stories evolve, the photographs fade. We're all hobbled together. Odds and ends. Bric-a-brac. CJ is: a buried body, Stocking talk, newspapers, videos and pictures, Raven's account, a diary. I can't put him back together. I can't put myself back together. The pieces are me but not mine.

2

A month prior to that dinner at the Stockings, I had written to Henry Joseph Raven, using the pseudonym John Dark. This was the failure from the ashes of which my new plan would grow.

I remember that first encounter with Raven the way one remembers meeting one's sweetheart, with fondness, and with a desire to go back and do it all over again. It was one of those unusually warm nights in Our Little Hamlet by the Sea; the temperature seemed to rise after the sun had gone down, and a fecund breeze perfumed the air. This, after an unremarkable muggy day. Patty was off at work; I had the house to myself. I'd discovered that the state maintained a complete database of prison inmates, accessible to anyone with an internet connection, and I had logged on to it. The house was quiet save the cats tumbling in the other room.

I clicked through some of the other captured convicts before I got to Raven—I knew he would be there and the anticipation was something I felt like drawing out. I saw men and women,

White, Black, Latino, Asian, all of them looking poor and poorly rested, defeated—though a few tried on a mask of defiance. Their crimes were listed along with their names and some other information, but the names of the crimes, *murder, manslaughter, assault with a deadly weapon*, provided little detail of their stories. You could stare at a picture long enough and imagine that plump, rosy-faced woman holding a gun under the counter and asking for all the money in the register, but since her story wasn't there, you couldn't be sure that was how it had happened. You were stuck with *armed robbery*. Shown a few in isolation, you might guess these individuals were victims of human rights violations, women who had just given birth, or men in drug rehab centers. But en masse they were malefactors.

He was waiting for me by the time I got down to the Rs, and he did not disappoint. He had the appearance of a murderer. Not all the murderers did. You could see in the way his eyes glared at the camera that he had no respect for human life. He looked hungry and tired, like he had been dragged out of bed moments before the picture was taken—it made sense, he had been on the lam for a week before they tracked him down. His eye sockets looked like they'd had billiard balls pushed into them. He had the stubbly, slack-jawed mien of a criminal who has finally been caught.

I swept aside my papers and cleared a space on my desk. I wrote several letters, each more cruel than the last, in an attempt to express my rage at the man responsible for CJ's death, for ruining our lives, for replacing my wife with a grim shadow of her former self. After I'd torn up six drafts, I realized that a piece of hate mail was unlikely to wound him or even capture his attention. So without a clear plan, I wrote as neutral a letter as possible, asking Henry Joseph Raven to be my pen-pal.

Dear Mr. Raven,

My name is John Dark and I'm looking for someone behind bars to correspond with. I have many different interests and I'm involved with a lot of prisoners' rights causes. If you're looking for a friend or just want someone to write to, feel free to respond at your earliest convenience. I'm looking forward to hearing from you.

Sincerely,
John Dark

I took out a PO box down the street so he could reply without finding out who I was. Unless you have a fake ID, you have to sign up for a PO box under your own name. However, you are free to list names you want to receive mail under. I put John Dark on the list. Any mail coming to him, I was assured by a pimply faced clerk, would be delivered to my box. Also, he told me, I didn't have to write "PO Box" or "Box #" as part of the address. I could write "Suite 1492"—giving the impression that I was writing from an actual room in an actual building.

I waited five days before checking the PO box. That would give my letter two days to get there, Raven a day to reply, and two days for his letter to make its way to me. There is no worse feeling than to open a mailbox and find it empty. Every day I would convince myself that Raven's response had been slipped into the slot of my mailbox, and that it was waiting there for me. I'd race to the mailbox, practically knocking people out of the way, pop open the box with my shiny little key and find . . . nothing. Day after day of nothing.

Then, one evening, an envelope. My heart was racing as I reached into the box and retrieved my paper quarry. Disappointment. A packet of coupons. Herald of the junk to come: Have You Seen This Child?, Amazing Grace Realty Wants to Sell You a Dream Home, Join our CD Club, Save the Children, Save the Animals, Save the Trees, Save the Earth, Save the Air. Addressed to Resident! The mail was coming in fine, just not from Henry Joseph Raven. I should reiterate that I had no actual plan as to how to respond to his response, if I were to get one. I trusted that I could improvise a way to make him pay for the suffering he had caused the Stockings. But the more I thought about it, the less I wanted to get a response, because I could not devise any way other than venting my anger, which was unlikely to affect him.

After three weeks, I closed down the PO box. My anxiety about Raven's not writing back to John Dark was displaced by a need to figure out how to tell Patty what I had done. I had never kept secrets from her, and I felt that somehow, in my failure, I needed to unburden myself. I took the day off from work to coincide with one of Patty's "weekends"—she had Wednesdays and Thursdays off. We walked down to our local park. The marine layer hadn't quite come in as far as our part of town, resulting in cool afternoon sunshine with half-clear skies. The park was full of kids, most of them in the playground section—"No Adults

Admitted Without Company of Children"—or by the dried-out fish pond. The empty concrete oval was full of young skateboarders trying their tricks.

The fish pond used to be full of water. I saw it once, as a teenager. I had spent the night in the park, after having taken the bus as far as it would take me away from my aunt and uncle's house. I remember wondering, before the police found me, how long I could survive eating the fish that swam around in there.

We made our way toward the middle of the diminutive park, to a patch of grass on which we could play Frisbee. Patty wore black sweatpants and a black t-shirt. We had just started playing. She was not very good at throwing, and I was not very good at catching; in the other direction, we achieved marvelous things. We had begun playing Frisbee because we were looking for an outdoor activity that didn't require much talking. We hated to sit around the house, and we'd grown tired of buying something every time we went out. We weren't joggers, golfers, cyclists, rollerbladers, surfers, volleyballers, softballers, basketballers, footballers, or any other kind of ballers, and—despite its aesthetic appeal—I hated tennis. I hated tennis because you could never know ahead of time whether courts would be available. We had tried target shooting for a while, with a Glock we bought for protection. I am a crack shot. I thought shooting would be good for Patty, but aside from the momentary thrill, it had no effect on her. Eventually, the local gun club was shut down because some depressed person decided to shoot himself instead of the target.

Frisbee was freedom. And aesthetically, Frisbee was pleasing, especially when I was throwing and she was catching. The other way around, aesthetics was lost in the dirt. There was something undeniably pleasurable about playing Frisbee with Patty, at a time when pleasure seemed in short supply. The combination of tranquility and exertion, the physicality of the exchange, the fact that we faced each other as we played.

I threw a long coasting shot that cleared her head and hovered there. She turned and plucked it from the air and faced me, all in one fluid motion. It's difficult to forget, more difficult to remember. She threw back, less gracefully.

I had decided that I would tell her that evening, over dinner, how I had rented the PO box and written to Henry Joseph Raven. I knew it would take a long time for her to understand what I had done. I would have to confess how misguided I'd been in trying to pursue correspondence with Raven. Digging the Frisbee from a hedge, I considered the possibility of never telling her what I had done. No, I had to come clean. Otherwise I would be able to think of little else. I was not well-suited to deception. I decided again that I would tell her over dinner, and I threw the Frisbee.

She caught it magnificently and returned it to me with a fluid and direct shot. The Frisbee drifted on the air as if in slow-motion. I skipped to the side and lined myself up to catch it. I crouched, raised my hands. Then the Frisbee, cruising directly through the frame of my outstretched fingers, hit me squarely on the forehead, and I had the idea. A plan to eclipse all plans dropped egg-like into my brain, whole, and it began with this realization: my pseudonym had been of the wrong gender. Why would Raven have any interest whatsoever in corresponding with John Dark? He was a lonely man, locked up with a bunch of other lonely men. He didn't need letters from another lonely man, on the outside, to add to his pile of loneliness and maleness. He needed a lonely woman.

The plan unfolded with crystal clarity in my mind even as I bent down to retrieve the Frisbee and throw it back to my wife. I would rent a new PO box under a female pseudonym. Henry Joseph Raven would fall in love with his correspondent and then, when she had wholly gained his affection, when she had come to inhabit every fiber of his being, she would break his heart. Raven would suffer the wrenching removal of someone from his life.

I resolved then and there not to tell Patty about my plan until I had reaped its fruits. The idea of hiding something from her, as I mentioned above, made me uncomfortable, but what I was doing I was doing for her, and when the opportunity came to reveal what I had done, that is, when my plan was successful, I'd tell her. All my duplicity would turn out for the best, like planning a surprise party. This was the only way I could unpoison the soil, restore a sense of justice and balance to our world, bring the old Patty back. Then we could begin building our normal lives again.

3

I got a new PO box, at the Mailboxes Store in Second City, a neighboring town, so Raven wouldn't suspect that John Dark and his new female correspondent were the same person. Composing the letter was simple enough. Naming her was the hard part. I went through hundreds of options before landing on lonely, lethal Lily Hazelton. Hazel-eyed Hazelton, Lily the lily, a trumpet on a slender stem. An invitation for Raven to tend or pluck. Then a haze, the magician's puff of smoke, and she's gone. Finally, a ton of bricks falls on his head. I'd woven the whole plan into the name—there was no way to lose sight of it.

I typed the letter on our old Olivetti and signed it in the most feminine way possible.

Dear Mr. Raven,

Are you looking for a pen-pal? My name is Lily

Hazelton and I am interested in writing back-and-forth with an incarcerated man.

Sincerely,
Lily Hazelton

The slight scraping sound the envelope made as it slid into the mailbox, the almost inaudible paper-on-paper kiss as it joined the other letters inside—I remember exactly dropping that first letter into the slot, remember thinking that I was, for the first time in a long time, for the first time ever, I should say, embarking on something truly important, not just a job, or a task, or a lark, but a mission. Few are lucky enough to find themselves a mission in our precious little time between womb and tomb. Now I have nothing but time and no courage to end time. They won't let me have my papers, but I can remember everything.

Patty and I were set up by a college friend of mine, Lennon Kwan. The pellucid waters of Lake Tahoe, the pellucid intentions of Lennon Kwan. Though Lennon and I took classes on opposite sides of campus—I majored in English, he in molecular biology—we spent a great deal of extracurricular time together. After college, he moved to San Francisco and I stayed in Los Angeles. We kept in touch as best we could.

I had a job but otherwise my life was a disaster. My friends in Los Angeles had long given up on me. I lived in a squalid 1950s apartment down by the beach. I drank myself to sleep most nights. The bright sunny weather was an affront. The outside world refused to reflect my inner world. I came to realize that not everyone had this problem. I considered daily the ways in which I might stitch myself back onto society. Everyone around me built lives with blithe unconcern for the fact that these same lives would crumble to bits one day. Some nights I slept outdoors, on the roof of my building. I highly recommend sleeping outdoors as a means of building one's character. It reminds one how the simple act of sitting inside an apartment watching daytime television actually reflects man's victory over the forces of nature.

Around this time, Lennon called me and asked if I was interested in joining him and a few friends on a Lake Tahoe ski trip. He had called me in the past, asking me to go on trips like this, and I had always refused. The Owen he was asking was not the Owen I had become. This time I decided to accept the invitation.

Upon my arrival in Tahoe I realized that the trip was not only about old friends getting back together. Everyone was a couple. Even Lennon had brought a date. The only exception, besides myself, was a large-eyed young woman with pale skin, the kind of skin that, with dark hair, looks translucent. She seemed unenthusiastic about me. I expected her to progress from lack of enthusiasm to disgust when she realized that I was the man with whom she was being set up in a sort of mutual-friend ambush. But shaking my hand, she smiled and said that she'd heard so much about me. How had she heard so much about me? I had heard nothing about her. I repressed the urge to mumble "likewise" and smiled back. Her name was Patricia Stocking. Patty. P. S. Like the Palm Springs bumper sticker: *P.S. I Love You,* and the license plate I saw once on Palm Canyon Drive: *PSIH8U.* We would love or hate each other.

New love should blossom under blue skies among explosive S-turns of fresh white powder, and maybe it does. But that week the weather seemed more conducive to no love. The first days alternated between gray gloom and blizzard, and the second half of the week brought a patchy cloudiness that melted snow only to reconstitute it as ice a half hour later.

She and I teamed up from the start. It was as straightforward as yelling "single!" in the line for the chairlift. She was a poor skier, unsteady on her legs, and could manage, at best, a wide sweeping snowplow down the bunny slope, knees bent enough so one couldn't say she wasn't bending her knees. I was an above average skier, and having had advance warning of her inexperience, I rented a snowboard to place myself further back on the learning curve. She wore a puffy lavender ski suit and white-framed mirror sunglasses. I wore jeans—my idea of fashion on the slopes—and by noon the seat of my pants was a frozen plate.

On the chairlift, she was a scientist. She pointed out dying trees and speculated about what had happened to them. She remarked on detail after detail of our surroundings, then hypothesized about why things were the way they were. While we glided smoothly above the trees—with a punctuating *pah-rump* each time we passed a tower—she talked about what she wanted to research when she got home. She had a pencil and notepad in her ski suit. She couldn't resist writing things down to look up later. That curiosity, her need to categorize and figure things out, belonged only to the old Patty. It would not last. When she pulled her hand out of her glove, it looked wrinkled and red, the skin of a newborn.

On the day of the blizzard, she wanted to keep skiing, even after I thought inclement weather might force us to cut the day short. The air was snow. Her technique never improved, her speed never increased, but she was having the time of her life, and while howling winds caused the chairlift to shut down periodically, she displayed no fear whatsoever. It was an amazing combination, this fearlessness coupled with a total inability to improve her skills. It would not last.

When she wasn't smiling or laughing, there was something severe about her face; mostly she looked sad. Like she'd been up all night arguing. Whatever attracted me to her appeared before I got to know her at all. And I met every new detail with rapacious enthusiasm. She could have told me she had six toes on each foot and I would have found in that fact two more reasons to love her. She was a rule follower but not a crowd follower. Her curiosity about the natural world often caused her attention to stray from what someone was saying—a condition I later dubbed *naturalist-autism*.

Her little house—which would become our little house—was as sweet and put-together as my apartment was not, but when I made her dinner at my place, she politely pretended that I did not live in a dump.

"I've seen worse," she said. "It's a bachelor pad."

"Sorry it's such a mess," I said. "I usually sleep on the roof anyway."

She laughed at this.

"When the weather's good," I clarified.

She laughed some more.

I had never thought of myself as funny. Yet there I was, making a beautiful woman laugh as I cooked her dinner. It was one of Patty's little talents, in those halcyon days, her ability to make me feel charming while I was only being myself.

"After you've fed me," she said, "we'll go sleep at my house."

I never slept at the apartment again.

The courtship phase has to occur correctly if the relationship is going to have any chance of lasting. An uninterrupted honeymoon, for example. Once we're into those plateau years, we have to keep drawing on the memories of those early days— they are our mutual creation myth. I wanted nothing more than the great plateau of marriage, the silent calm of mature love.

A month later, I had it. We eloped, then had a reception at her parents' house. The Stockings lived in a California neo-colonial, meaning it looked like one of those East Coast houses on the outside, it carried that kind of visual authority, but if subjected to actual East Coast weather it would probably blow down. I found the house intimidating, both for its affluent surroundings and its blue-chip attitude—the way its columns and shutters repelled anything half-baked. I could feel which parts of myself forged on with confidence toward that house, and which parts wanted to turn around and run to the curb.

The tented yard was full of people I didn't know. My aunt and uncle were there, too, of course, but they were the only ones on the "groom's side." The Stockings introduced me around. These new people would surround me for the rest of my life. When I kissed Patty in front of them, I looked into her eyes and I thought, finally, I can rest. I am going to assemble a life for myself, and she is going to lead the way. It is amazing, though, how you can be watching something for a long time, and it looks one way, then the light shifts a little, or the wind blows, and that branch is an insect. That rock is a fish. That owl's eye is a butterfly wing.

We had to rush home from Cabo San Lucas. Funeral, arrests, trial dates. For weeks, she cried herself to sleep. Then, without consulting me, she switched to the night shift. Her company was generating nasal-spray drugs around the clock and they needed quality-assurance people there all the time. She told me she would rather sleep during the day. I was patient—I had no other choice. There was no consoling her. At the beginning, at least, I tried to find happiness where I could.

Where we used to laugh over bygone injuries, we now cried over bygone pleasures. Our house, situated in the middle of the block, was the most peaceful place I had ever known. I spent hours on our wooden deck in back, reading the newspaper and watching the hummingbirds bob from flower to colorful flower. Gone. In the winter the air was brisk and refreshing, and we treated the occasional rainstorm as a rare event worth celebrating, by mixing cocktails and lighting a firelog. The crackle of wood, the tinny patter of rain on the metal plate of the air-conditioner . . . the night-blooming jasmine of February, the wild winds of April, the muggy fogs of June, the dry hot Septembers, the smell of brush fire smoke on the hot Santa Ana winds of October . . . all gone. Our Little Hamlet by the Sea belonged to one season alone, not the season of L.A. cliché, the season of no-season, but the season of memory, all of the seasons superimposed upon each other, like a broth into which new elements were constantly added, so that something from long ago could bob up next to a brand new ingredient. Someday, all the elements would become lost in a single flavor. There were days on which our street would be filled with the harsh music of crows calling to each other from the treetops. I could never determine whether they were fighting or mating, but I could watch those sleek black birds call back and forth and chase each other for hours. Only later did I make the connection—those enormous black crows. Ravens. Every moment contains within it the seeds of its own destruction.

4

I waited a week to check the new PO box. I didn't think Raven would respond. I drove over to the Mailboxes Store in Second City. There was a personal letter in my box. I opened it.

Dear Ms. Hazelton,

I would like a new pen pal. Please send a picture.
Signed,
Henry Joe

Patty and I on our honeymoon were like any happy young couple on a honeymoon. We drank tropical drinks, lazed around the beach, stared at each other over fussy dinners, and made love when we felt like it. We stayed in a cottage, steps from the sand, isolated from but serviced by a large resort further up the beach.

It was utterly unlike the Spring Break images of Cabo San Lucas I'd seen on television. I was content to soak everything up quite passively, as I understood one was supposed to do, but Patty insisted on learning all the resort workers' names, and she pointed out, again and again, plants, sea life, and insects that had been all but invisible to me. This was what I had fallen in love with on the chairlift, and I loved her even more for it now. Maybe I can be like this, I thought. Maybe I can be open and curious and kind like this.

We had been there four days when she decided we should rent a jeep and explore the Sierra de la Laguna, the local mountain range. She wanted a nature fix. We had snorkeled the day before, but I'd gotten disoriented because of some problem with my inner ear. According to her guidebook, the local mountains hosted an astounding variety of indigenous flora and fauna. We had loaded up the jeep with some picnic gear and food, and we were pulling out of the hotel parking lot when Eduardo, the goateed, effeminate concierge, chased us down.

"Telefono, telefono," he said. "Emergencia."

I did not know what had happened, obviously, but we had reached one of those moments, Fate's forks, when in an instant our lives change completely.

Standing in the Mailboxes Store, looking at the short note signed "Henry Joe," I knew I'd reached another of Fate's forks. If I was going to move forward, I would have to create a picture of Lily. I didn't want to borrow images of a random woman and use her for my purposes. I wanted her to be her own person, an image that couldn't be traced back to anyone else. I didn't want to get trapped in some coincidence, or set Raven searching after some poor woman who had nothing to do with any of this.

When I am at a loss, I turn to the world of books. The library here is abysmal. Back in those halcyon days, a massive bookstore had just appeared a few blocks from our home, located in a building that had once housed a massive pet store, then a massive clothing store, then a massive audio-video store. A sun-faded banner hanging over the old audio-video store sign identified the place as "GBS Books," the GBS standing for "Giant Book Sale," inscribed on the tattered street-level banners. It was an enormous remainder depot, a book pound, where literature was adopted and taken home or put to sleep forever. The place was populated by two bitter staffers (one absorbed in a massive science-fiction tome), a crying child in the Children's Corner, and a pee-smelling older woman making her way through the stack of expired calendars, one page at a time.

That was where I found *Photoshop Secrets for Everyone*. It described all of the various filters and techniques one could use to assemble futuristic photo collages, change backgrounds, "airbrush" away wrinkles, make fat people look thinner, even make someone look like someone else entirely. I took the book home and reviewed it thoroughly. The information was useful, but the prose was limp and, at times, unclear. I would not want my name on such a book.

Now to source material. Where could I find generic images of regular women? I spent some time browsing through stock photography catalogues on the internet. I couldn't find anything that looked enough like a casual snapshot. I had better luck with an image search engine. I tried several different searches: "snapshot," "woman," "young woman," "female," "normal woman," "Jane Doe," "Annabelle," and so on, with limited success.

The magic words, it turned out, were "just me." Something about the humility of that phrase yielded a great number of straightforward, unprofessional pictures of average-looking women, along with a variety of pictures of overweight men, prom singles, pornography, and people with their pets ("just me with my cats").

Using the alchemical Photoshop, I created a composite Lily Hazelton that could not be traced back to any single individual. Lily sits on an overturned aluminum Grumman canoe, wearing short jean-shorts and a yellow tank top. She looks directly at the camera, smiling coyly—what a labor of pixels that was—and wields a paddle in her hands. Her nipples, thanks to a distortion trick, are slightly erect under the fabric of her tank top. A headband holds her straight sandy brown hair in place. She's attractive, a little mysterious, outdoorsy but clean, and she's just a touch out of focus.

I had no idea what kind of woman Henry Joseph Raven would like. Lily looked wholesome but adventurous. I followed my gut when it came to piecing together her features. Only when I was finished, putting the picture into the envelope along with a note (below), did I notice that the Lily Hazelton still hovering on my screen looked like my cousin Eileen might have looked if she were still alive.

Dear Mr. Raven,

Here is a picture of me from a recent canoe trip. I thought something from the out-of-doors would be fun. I look forward to writing back and forth with you.

Sincerely,
Lily Hazelton

Patty was my second true love. Her impossible predecessor: my cousin Eileen. Would I have fallen in love with Eileen had we not been placed under the same roof? I've thought about it endlessly, and I believe she could have pierced my heart even had we grown up on opposite sides of town. She was older, haughty, worldly, and despite our propinquity, always distant. She had developed from an early age a sense of the theatrical, and she had created an aura about herself, which she maintained seemingly without effort. Every once in a while, though, I could feel one eye trained on me, to see how I was taking it all in, to make sure she was still on top. When I moved in with my aunt and uncle, she treated me more like a houseguest or a nuisance than a new younger sibling. It was an ideal arrangement. I was close enough to feed the flames of my love; she was too distant to extinguish them.

One day things changed. I was thirteen, she was sixteen. I was in my bedroom, on my bed, examining a *Playboy* magazine I'd smuggled from my uncle's collection for temporary use. The house was deserted. My aunt and uncle had gone to a convention and weren't supposed to return until nightfall, and Eileen was rehearsing a class project at a friend's house. I took the opportunity to liberate my self-pleasuring activity from the confines of the tiny bathroom (fan on, water running) and enjoy myself in the *plein air* of my bedroom (music on, shorts off). I lay there, wad of tissue at ready, stroking myself with one hand, flipping pages with the other, trying to make the moment last, when my door swung open.

Eileen appeared in the doorway, smiling. I panicked, pulled sheets over myself, groaned in horror, and all the while the image of her smile burned itself into the back corner of my brain. This was not a smile of embarrassment, nor a smile of pleasure at my embarrassment, but a smile of calm, concentrated desire. She appeared at the end of my bed. I told her to go away. She shook her head, still with that smile on her face. The door, I noticed, had gotten re-closed in her wake. Then, as she moved toward me, she uttered a phrase I will never forget: "Let me help you, Owen."

I was her first boyfriend. We were mildly ashamed at our being cousins and being together; nevertheless, it was a secret well kept from the rest of the family. She alternated between aggression and shyness. She wanted or didn't want certain things to happen. I was too young and inexperienced to know where we were heading next, so I always let her "drive." That was the language we used—she was old enough to drive, I wasn't. (Later, much later, I saw the play *How I Learned to Drive*, in which this metaphorical construct was pursued in telling the story of an uncle's initiation of his niece. I walked out, to Patty's disappointment.

Rather than explain any of it to her I faked stomach cramps for the next two and a half hours and pretended to vomit in our locked bathroom, pouring cup after cup of water into the toilet while retching intermittently.)

Eileen and I kept it up for a summer, at the end of which we were discovered. My aunt and uncle were horrified. There was talk about sending me back to live with my father, but it was decided that Eileen and I had learned our lesson. They would keep their eyes on us. My aunt didn't trust my father. A few months later, Eileen got herself a boyfriend, some eleven years her senior.

I moped for a while, couldn't untangle my feelings, chased various other girls who reminded me of her. She moved out a year and a half later. During my college years, Eileen lived in what she called an "artists' colony" and others called a "sober community center," but which was in fact a shooting gallery for addicts, and unlike any depiction of one I'd seen in movies or on television. I visited her there only once. Her room was in a lofted space, hidden behind a series of false bookshelves, and had no windows. She'd painted the walls bright colors and light came over the top of the bookshelves and down the angled ceiling. It was a tiny, cramped, cozy space which made me think of a camping tent. I didn't see any bathtub when I was there.

We went for a walk and an almost unrecognizable figure from my high school lagged just behind us. My cousin shouted expletives at him to go away. He had been the most talented— naturally talented—young pianist at my school and was now convinced we were going out to "score" and wanted in on it. Eileen and I had a cup of coffee down the street. She, who had been my sexual initiator, had lost all sense of sexuality about her person. She wanted money but didn't ask for it. I left her something to help her "get back on her feet" and gave her my phone number at the college. She never called.

Six months later, my aunt called to invite me to Eileen's funeral. She'd died, in the bathtub, of a drug overdose. I spoke with her friends and with other cousins, and I heard rumors that she had left a note. My aunt never mentioned any note. Perhaps she wanted to make it seem less her fault than willful suicide, or perhaps there never was a note and Eileen's death had actually been an accident. I never found myself able to ask.

The young woman lying in the coffin was both Eileen and not Eileen. I had not seen her for six months, and she'd been doing serious drugs; she bore little resemblance to the healthy pre-drug Eileen of a few years back. She was thinner, of course; her hair looked synthetic. Most people, upon encountering a corpse in a viewing room, look at the chest, for signs of breathing. On television, people walk up slowly and sadly or throw their bodies on the casket, but in real life most people, whether they admit it or not, look for a final sign that their loved one is really, truly dead.

Half a year earlier any trace of sexuality had been missing. In the casket, it was back, thanks to her mother picking out a dress from the days of clean Eileen, and thanks to a makeup artist who had probably mistaken her unhealthy looks as the pall of death and decided to restore her to a long-gone, fictional Eileen-hood that none of us who knew her had seen for years. Which is not to say she didn't look like a corpse. Her skin had lost its translucency (once prized by me) and had gone as opaque as a candle.

It wasn't until her funeral that I charted my cousin's appetite for self-destruction and linked it to the way she had treated me as a boy. I had always considered our summer to be my first legitimate encounter with the opposite sex, but looking back on it, I began to wonder where she had acquired the forwardness, the enormous sexual appetite that never seemed entirely her own. And so my experience of Eileen's funeral was one of scrutinizing the older men, relatives, and friends, for he who had been there first.

5

Raven's reply number two was brief:

Thanks for the picture. I jerked off to it.

HJR

I could almost hear him laughing.

The next morning, I kissed sleeping Patty goodbye and made my way over to the office, where I hoped I could forget about Lily a moment and get a few things accomplished. When Patty was asleep, a part of me was asleep.

Neil was sitting at my desk when I arrived. My cubicle had a window at one end, his did not, so I was not surprised to see him there in his usual Hawaiian shirt and navy blue pants. I was not surprised, either, to see my trash can stuffed with the remains of his fast-food breakfast.

"Out," I said.

"Sorry, man. Hang on a sec. Let me just save these docs."

"Quickly," I said. I stood behind him and looked out the plate glass window. It was dirty. "Did you leave those handprints on the window?"

"No."

"They weren't there when I was here a few days ago."

"Maybe you should come in more often."

"My wife is having a difficult time, remember? And I get more work done at home without you bothering me every five minutes. Now could you please clean the window?"

"I didn't get it dirty," he said. He held his hand up to the glass to show me that the handprints did not match. "Probably someone's kids."

"Did you bring your kids in here?"

"Nope."

"Could you at least take your trash when you go?"

He did.

I pulled my files out of my bag and got ready to work on them, but found I could not concentrate. I fetched myself some coffee. Neil snacked and breathed, I felt murderous. Every time I looked up, I saw a child's greasy handprints blocking my view of the office park. I am not by nature a neat person, but I do like a clean working environment. I called down to maintenance and asked them to send someone up to wipe away the handprints. They summoned a sympathetic janitor who sprayed and squee-geed the window clean.

I got in a solid four hours' work on the software manual be-fore Raven crept into my consciousness again. Lily had managed to tap one avenue of appetite, and Raven had responded. He hadn't seen through my ruse. It was a start. But did Raven really mean to dismiss such an eager correspondent? Either he was trying to test Lily in some way or he had succumbed to one of those destructive impulses so common to the criminal mind. It seemed to me he could have milked a real Lily Hazelton for more pictures before testing her tolerance for obscenity. This line of thinking brought me to the conclusion that the "test model" was not necessarily the most likely explanation. I leaned toward the "impulse model." The same brain chemistry that would allow someone to kill another human being without thinking about the consequences might also move him to "kill" a correspondence without considering the deleterious effects it would have on future contacts.

When I was a child, I took one of my favorite records—a happy song about sunshine and sidewalks—and placed it between my mattress and the boxspring. By jumping up and down on the bed repeatedly, I managed to quietly smash it to bits. I have often wondered why I did that. I never told anyone. I threw the record away in the trash cans behind the house. I was too young to buy another copy, and I did not want to tell my father what I had done, so I never heard the song again. To this day, I can only remember that it was about sunshine and sidewalks. I composed the next letter, window glass clean and Neil gone for the night, with pen and paper, to be typed up at home while Patty was at work.

Dear Henry,

I can understand how lonely you must be in there and for that reason I will overlook the somewhat crude tone of your most recent letter.

Maybe you thought I was not going to respond to it. And maybe I shouldn't have. But there's something about you that makes me want to write again.

Sometimes, in the middle of the day, when I'm unloading groceries or putting on my heels for a night out, I wonder what you're doing. This past week, I imagined you were looking at my picture. I felt the strangest feeling of connection, like I was thinking about you while you were thinking about me. Did you feel it too?

Lily

PS Do you have any pictures of yourself besides the one on the D.O.C. Web site?

When one considers what one has lost in life, the things one really misses above and beyond everything else are totally unexpected. If asked back then what I would miss, I would have said: 1. Walking with Patty. 2. Sex with Patty. 3. Our house. 4. The ocean, though I'd always liked it more as an idea than something to swim around in.

What I actually miss the most, judging by how my mind turns to it again and again through no operation of my will: walking into our bedroom in the middle of the day and watching Patty sleep. At the start I did it absent-mindedly, checking on her to make sure she was okay, refilling her water glass if she'd emptied it. I moved as quietly as possible, not daring to disturb her slumber. Occasionally, I pulled up a chair and sat by the bed, watching her face. People always claim they can tell when they're being watched, but Patty was not one of those people. Sometimes her eyes moved back and forth under her eyelids in REM. I listened to her breathing in the silence of the afternoon. I wondered what she might be dreaming about. Oh what I would give now to hear the quiet whistle of air coursing in and out of her nose. To watch her flip from her back onto her side, from her side onto her stomach. Fingers tugging at the sheets.

She reminded me of the Patty I'd seen in pictures on her parents' mantle, pictures from her youth and teenage years. I was always drawn to those pictures. I imagined myself knowing her back then. In Patty's sleeping face I was able to glean the innocence of her youth. Something else came over her face when she was awake, when she was in time. Asleep, her face lost all trace of fear and concern. I felt honored to have the opportunity to witness that transformation. My love for her was refreshed by it. Only later did I realize that the governing factor in the transformation of her sleeping face to her waking face was not being in time versus outside time, but putting on and carrying the awareness that her brother had been removed from her life.

"In dreams," she told me, "CJ sometimes shows himself. I get confused. I tell him I thought he was dead. And he smiles and tells me he didn't really die. He tells me he faked the funeral. He comes up with any number of reasons why. To get away from my parents, for a laugh, because someone was after him . . . I believe it, every time."

"The same thing happens to me," I said. "With my cousin Eileen. But I've trained myself to recognize the dream as a dream."

6

I tried not to check the PO box for a week. It was the only way I could maintain control over the situation. Besides, I didn't want to have to drive to Second City every day. I had work to attend to. Near the end of the self-imposed week I ended up at the Mailboxes Store on a day when I should have been at the office.

I practiced, as I turned the key in the mailbox lock, a steadiness of emotion. Sliding the key in, feeling the tumblers, I turned myself into that same metal out of which the box was constructed. The hope, the anxiety—all of it I learned to quell. I knew that I would have to harden my heart even as I devised a way to seduce Mr. Raven, that this would be no precise shot from a guard tower but an intimate embrace concluding with a shank to the entrails.

The mailbox was empty.

The store was run by a man and a woman. I don't know if they were brother and sister or husband and wife, but they shared the same last name on their business cards. I asked the wife/sister behind the counter if any large packages had come, anything too big to fit into the mailbox.

"No, nothing."

My tires squealed on the way out of the Mailboxes Store parking lot—my foot expressing my frustration, my ears surprised to hear about it—and I pulled into an inexplicable knot of midday traffic. No sirens, no construction, no special event—just cars and trucks in my way in every direction. And the sun, so bright and optimistic before I'd gone in, had now taken on a orange cast. Damn the shortening of days! I found myself caught in the grip of time-anxiety. Another day going by: I am going to die. One day I'm going to die, and when that day comes, if I'm unlucky enough to be conscious, I'm going to wish I could have back this half-hour in utterly pointless traffic. And then, blaming myself: If only I had written to Raven as Lily in the first place, I could be doing this from down the street, in our town, instead of way out here in Second City. How many more trips would I make? One for every letter, probably, plus days like today when I would jump the gun. Or, and this more than anything turned out to be the primary source of my anxiety, maybe Raven was already done with Lily. Maybe he would never write back.

I crept along, watching others lose patience on the road, honking and yelling at each other, and I managed to find a way out of my anxiety into a calmer state. There is nothing like the sight of someone else losing his cool to make one feel serene and calm. I noticed this in arguments. The more irrational Patty got, the more rational I would become, until she would accuse me of being either insensitive or not "on her team," which would develop a second-tier argument, the subject of which—independent from the first-tier argument—was always the immutability of my character flaws.

People honking. Owen in Zen-like calm despite time-anxiety and Raven-anxiety. Calm enough to venture a trip to the market, having just realized, a block from the house, that we were out of milk, cat litter, and various other things essential to the smooth running of our household. I say "calm enough" for the market because markets have always inspired in me a feeling of dread. The supermarket is a one-stop shop for everything edible, representing freedom from the bonds of subsistence, or from time-consuming trips to multiple merchants. Acquiring food from such a place makes me feel as though I have become fully detached from any sort of natural world. This is not uncommon, I'm sure, and this thought probably hovers around the packaged meat section like a fly, waiting to pop into people's heads. Plus there is the massiveness of supermarkets, the recognition that one has entered a very dense territory for which one does not have a map. Not to mention the housewives, piloting their carts as they do their giant truck-cars, with abandon and entitlement. And then there is the strange primal phenomenon by which we view unfamiliar-named supermarkets as somehow suspect, evidence to my mind that we form subtle subconscious bonds to our local supermarkets, and do so solely out of familiarity, to the extent that anything that is not Pavilion's or Gelson's seems untrustworthy. We form relationships with giant corporate food warehouses as if they were the local butcher, smiling at us from above his blood-spattered apron.

Our local market was smaller than a supermarket and inspired proportionally less dread. Still I viewed everyone there with suspicion, especially the rich older women who shopped with their sunglasses on. Patty thought they did it to hide bad eye-jobs. I was not so sure.

I had begun experimenting with sunglasses myself, testing the theory that my dread might have stemmed from having to make eye contact with too many unfamiliar people. (I detest festivals too, though they don't require as much eye contact because you're not negotiating a shopping cart through tight spaces and blind turns.) I wore a pair of gold-framed, mirror-lensed aviator's glasses into the market. The first time I had done this I had found my dread decreased significantly. Though maybe I was so busy thinking about the effect of the shades, the dread couldn't enter my consciousness. It was hard to see at first, but my eyes adjusted eventually. I'd avoided the mistake of colored lenses—many of the products familiar to us are recognized by color.

I retrieved a cart from the line of carts and proceeded to shop, loading up with coffee, eggs, milk, kitty litter, and so on. I was in the massive apple section, scanning the astounding number of varieties—Fuji, Gala, Red Delicious, Golden Delicious, Braeburn, Cameo, Pink Lady, Jonagold, Granny Smith, McIntosh, Rome, Criterion—when I heard a woman's voice.

"Owen?" Patty's mother. She was not wearing sunglasses. She appraised herself briefly in my mirror-shades, after which she waited for me to remove them, which I would not do.

"Hi Minerva," I said, with an exaggerated peer into her cart, "what's for dinner?"

"You know to call me Minnie," she said. She smiled and answered my question. Pork chops with applesauce. After some chit-chat, during which my glasses seemed to become more of a mystery to her, as opposed to something to get used to, she said: "Oh—I wanted to tell Patricia about this, but I'll tell you first. The most amazing thing happened to me this afternoon, just before I drove here, actually."

She paused, waiting for me to say "uh-huh," which I did.

She tilted from side to side as if trying to peer around my shades. I was tempted to remove them, to make her feel more comfortable, but I didn't want to mess with my experiment and so left them on. Now I imagine it from her perspective, dodging her own reflection, back and forth, while she told me the following. I remember it verbatim.

"I was trying to decide what to cook tonight, and I was absent-mindedly looking out the window at that big maple in our front yard, you know the one?"

I nodded.

"The wind was rippling the leaves and it was kind of pretty, so I kept my eyes on it for a second or two. Nothing I hadn't seen before, really, but it was like Something said to me: 'Stop, wait. Appreciate the moment.' You know?"

"Sure," I said. I thought she was about to ask me to take off the sunglasses, but she didn't.

"And so I watched the tree a little longer than I would have and you know what happened?"

I shook my head.

"A single leaf dropped. Just one. No leaves on the ground, mind you, and no others falling. I waited. No others fell. And I knew it was Calvin Junior checking in." She waited.

I nodded.

"Reminding me to appreciate my life. Just because one leaf falls, he was telling me, doesn't mean the whole tree does too. A subtle message, for sure, but he always was the subtle one."

"Sounds to me like he understood symbolism really well." This wasn't quite enough, so I added: "It's always nice to get a message."

"It sure is," she said.

If I could get in a time machine and go back to that moment, I would add the following: "You think you're the recipient, Minerva, but you're really the messenger."

7

Exactly one week after checking the mailbox and finding it empty, I returned to find a letter inside from Henry Joseph Raven. The delay, it turned out, had been occasioned by his tracking down and forwarding to Lily a photo of himself, pre-incarceration, a photo which slipped out of the envelope onto my lap in the Mailboxes Store parking lot.

In his mug shot, Raven had looked like someone dragged out of bed, and his bleary-eyed stare was both murderous and bored—a cold-blooded combo. So when I received this new photograph from him, an older photo, from the outside, I was caught off guard by how handsome and alert and full of life he appeared, standing in front of an old but shiny pickup truck. I was surprised by the total disappearance of any criminality from his face—that murderer look was nowhere in evidence. Notwithstanding that the picture was probably taken before he killed CJ, there was nothing of the criminal about Henry Joseph Raven. He had taken care to comb his dark hair and his cheeks were fresh and ruddy from shaving. He didn't look as gaunt and poor as he had in the mug shot. He and his environs were clearly working-class—red-checked flannel, blue jeans with a belt, work boots—but all of it was very neat, and one got the impression that the image had been taken to celebrate some special occasion, the repainting of his pickup truck, perhaps.

He stood before a 1970s Dodge, candy-apple red, clean. The sky was clear and blue, and the light was crisp, accentuated by the sharp edges of the leafless trees. A nest revealed by the loss of foliage was lodged in the fork of two branches. A green shed in the background marked the edge of the image. On the other side of the shed the ground dropped away as toward a creek. Hills above, then just through the treetops, mountains. Mountains to the west, the sun above them but not too far gone, casting Raven and his truck into muted light compared to the brighter beams hitting the female photographer, whose reflected image was discernible in the pickup's shiny surface.

I studied the photograph, figured out when it was most likely taken, learned about the truck (no license plate visible) and the shed. I tried to take two dimensions and turn them into three, to hunt the geography that matched the image in my head. I tried—how I tried—but most of the time I ended up staring aimlessly into that 4 x 6 inch world, trying to extract from Raven's image some shard of understanding. And even back then, sitting in the car outside the Mailboxes Store, photograph up on the steering wheel, even then I felt toward the female reflection in a red pickup a pang of jealousy on behalf of my Lily Hazelton.

Miss Hazelton,

I was surprised to get your letter. I thought I had scared you off for sure. Let me explain a few things:

1. I did not actually do what I said I did in my letter to you.
2. I am an upstanding individual and do not make it my policy to lie to people especially strangers and women but some circumstances beyond my control led me to write that letter to you. They were:
   a. I was at the time (but am no longer) corresponding with only one female on the outside who is no longer my fiancée due to other circumstances beyond my control. Therefore I was not in need of new correspondents.
   b. Lots of females seem to think they can start up correspondence and drop it whenever. Your picture made me think that you were one of them. Least I could do for myself and other incarcerated males was scare you off.
   c. In addition to (a) and (b) I had a good laugh over it. It is hard to stay entertained in here.
3. It is a promising thing that you don't scare so easy.
4. I have sent you a picture too so now we are even. Some other things you should know:
   a. I am not stupid.
   b. I am a decent man.

5. If you are out to save me or convert me in any religious way stop now.

Regards

HJR

I was working on Lily's response a few evenings later when I heard shuffling outside my home office door. At first, I thought it was one of the cats, wanting to come in. The cats always acted crazy after the sun went down. I rose from my desk and opened the door. Patty looked like she had been about to knock.

"Come in," I said. I slid a pile of books off the daybed. "Have a seat."

She entered but did not sit. "Are you going to be working much longer?"

I shook my head. "Almost done." A letter I would later throw away—one of many throw-away drafts, not meant for Raven's eyes, but rather to form a subtext for Lily—sat waiting in the typewriter. My plan for the rest of the night's work consisted of feeding it to the wastebasket.

"Then I'll get the movie," she said. "Will you be done by the time I get back?"

"Sure." I had forgotten that it was Wednesday. Patty didn't have to go to work.

She seemed almost ready to leave the room but moved toward my desk. It was covered with stacks of paper, printouts of software manual pages, random notes, pens and pencils, along with the computer, and to one side, the Olivetti typewriter with the letter in it. Patty scanned these at a reasonable distance, close enough to indicate her curiosity, far enough away to acknowledge my privacy.

"You're using the typewriter?"

"I like to make noise while I'm working."

She moved toward the typewriter.

"Hey Patty," I said. "If you want me to show you what I'm working on, I will."

She stepped back immediately. "No, no, no. I'm sorry I even came in here."

"Some exciting stuff here about using spreadsheets."

"I'm sorry. What movie should I get?"

"I don't know. Something funny."

"New or old?"

"Old. You're just getting one?"

"Probably a few." She closed the door on her way out.

No good-bye kiss, no sense that she wanted to spend her evening curled up in my arms without the blue glow of a television in front of us. A few movies. She was going to stay up all night again. Sleep all day.

How I wanted to be able to show Patty something then, to let her know what I was doing for her! I wanted to be like the cat who drops a bird on the doorstep. I couldn't wait to show her my little bird—my big bird, my Raven—and what I had done to him. She would finally understand the depth of my devotion to her, and to what she did not seem capable of: restoring her to her former self.

The next morning, I was back at it.

Dear Henry,

I want you to feel like you cannot live without me, and then I want you to live without me.

I couldn't send that to Raven—it was practically a thesis statement. I had to draw him in, to make him want to seduce my Lily, to plant a seed in his head. Unfortunately, a planted seed gives no confirmation of its planting until much later. In the meanwhile, the essence of the thing was to keep up the illusion, to maintain the dream of Lily Hazelton as seamlessly as possible.

I tried to be an actor for a while, in high school. Not because I was a particularly good student of human behavior, or a great lover of the theater, but because I wanted everyone to admire me, to recognize me for what I had done on the stage. Luckily, I figured out early that I was not an actor, and so did not have to deal with later failure and re-evaluation of my life's goal, as several of my fellow drama club members had to do. But in high school, before I had come to that realization, I auditioned for every play. Our director, while hardly blind to which kids were talented and which were not, would on occasion reward those who had done good work on the technical crews a decent part in one of the upcoming plays.

The bone thrown me was Lysander in *A Midsummer Night's Dream*. Late one night we were rehearsing out-of-doors in our

Little Epidaurus by the Sea. Someone—I can't remember who—was supposed to walk up behind Lysander and surprise him. Time after time, with the director trying strategy after strategy, I failed to register any semblance of the human reaction known as surprise. I tried to "feel" surprised—it didn't work. I tried to "feel" unaware, so that I would then "be" surprised—didn't work either. Finally, recognizing that I would not be able to spur a subconscious reaction via these conscious means, I did my best to "mimic" surprise, and the result was so ham-fisted, it earned a restrained chuckle from the audience every night, a result which I considered better than nothing. My career as an actor began as ham-fisted mimicry and became, as I took myself more seriously, constipatedly minimalist. I excised everything that did not seem natural and ended up with nothing at all.

The same thing was happening as I drafted my letters to Raven. By the time I had cut out everything artificial, everything ham-fisted and suspect, I ended up with a page of crossed-out sentences. I would have to move beyond mimicry if I wanted any chance of success.

8

After Patty slept the day away, she and I went to dinner at her friends' house, rich friends, about whose source of wealth we knew little. They had bought an enormous mansion in the hills. Their primary occupation seemed to be throwing dinner parties. For some reason along the way they had adopted Patty (and, by extension, me) into their circle and we would get invited occasionally to their table, at which sat an assortment of individuals and couples, specially selected to socialize well together, always with some new blood thrown in. Later, I discovered that our hostess kept a book in the kitchen in which she inscribed, for every dinner, the guests at the table, the food served, and who should be re-invited with whom and whether any glaring incompatibilities showed up.

We arrived early and therefore had to tolerate the most awkward stage of the evening, waiting for the other couples to arrive. Showing up late was Patty's preference—you could join in conversations that had already started, you could survey all the social dynamics in one swift appraising glance. But I could not stand being late. "You'd rather catch our hostess in curlers," Patty used to say, "than risk being the last to arrive."

I had been preoccupied with my response to Raven all day, and I had to make a conscious effort to reintegrate into the social world. Patty had not looked so elegant in a long time. She wore black, of course, but something about this outfit made her look as though she had decided to cast off the mourner's uniform for the night. With the right makeup and a good mood, her big eyes and natural sneer made her look like royalty. I had accepted, but never fully gotten used to, the way Patty could transform herself, depending on whether she was going to work, dinner, or a party—each place requiring a specific kind of performance—and I found myself looking forward to this evening, to observing her in her element. I felt lucky and proud that she was mine.

Patty and our hostess talked about each other's outfits while the host and I exchanged grumbling greetings, both of us acknowledging thereby that the evening belonged to the women, so to speak. The house was big and hollow and new, and while you could spot our hostess's attempts to make it cozy and homey—blankets thrown over the couches, flowers in the alcoves—the effect was one of attempted hominess rather than the genuine feeling anyone lived there.

Several more people arrived; we stood in the kitchen, sipping wine, making introductions. The room was broken up into several one-on-one or one-on-two conversations. I stood alone, occupying myself with the opening and pouring of wine, and sampled bits and pieces of what people were saying. One can learn a great deal by zipping the mouth and opening the ears. I watched the women, the way they handled the men. I am a quick study.

A current event absorbed, amoeba-like, all the other topics, and the small conversations became a big group conversation. There had been another suicide bombing in the Middle East. It had been all over the news that day. Dozens of people, many of them children, dead. The talk went round and round, with expressions of sympathy for the victims, shaking heads of halfway-around-the-world impotence, a few words about the news media, early symptoms of compassion-fatigue and its cousin, compassion-fatigue-fatigue. There is no group duller than one's peers.

"I cannot understand how someone would think it's a good idea to blow themselves up," said our host.

"And kill children," added our hostess. Various gestures of agreement.

"It's incomprehensible." This from a short and bearded Professor of Something.

"They're maniacs."

I hadn't said anything. I had been trying to cut the foil from a bottle of white wine with the sharp tip of the opener's corkscrew. I had not yet learned that most foil tops can be pulled right off, sleeve-like. You have to keep your eye on that sharp metal tip if you don't want to spear your finger and give yourself tetanus. I sliced the foil and removed it successfully.

"What I can't understand," I offered, "is why we think we're any different." I twisted the corkscrew into the cork. I had only meant to throw in my two cents, but now I had everyone's attention. "I mean, who's to say any one of us wouldn't do the same thing if placed in that situation?"

"I, for one, would not." The professor again.

"You don't know that for sure," I said.

"I think I do."

"Even if you were placed in the same environment—war, poverty, martyrdom the only heroism, no knowledge of another kind of life, no other options to make your mark?"

"In that case, friend, we're not talking about me anymore."

But others are like us.

Others are us.

They feel what we feel.

I was constructing my reply when Patty took the bottle from my hand. People stepped forward with their glasses. I watched her fill them. The prior conversations resumed in dyads and triads. And the professor? He was now engaged in golf-talk with our host.

Our hostess cleared her throat. "I hope everyone is hungry."

We were ten total around the table. The subject, once we were seated, shifted toward what we all did for a living, and in some cases, what we all wanted to be doing for a living. I might have preferred a discussion about what we were reading, but— as I had learned at an earlier dinner—not everyone reads for pleasure, and those who don't are ashamed of that fact, so discussions about books should occur only in the confines of a "book club"— to which I have never belonged.

The table was crowded with flowers, candles, napkins, plates, glasses (two each), and silverware. On each of our plates sat tiny sterling-silver pigs, into whose pigtails were tucked cards with our names laser-printed on them. The hostess had divided the couples, so that I found myself sitting across the table from Patty and two seats over. I tried to catch her eye now and then, give her a wink, which she indulged and admonished with a half-smile. She wanted me to act like an adult. I spoke with our hostess, mainly, about how good the food was, and listened to the other conversations around the table. A swirling conversational sinkhole. I was in a sour mood, I admit. Were I placed in that room today I might consider it paradise. But I am obliged to reproduce my attitude then, however lazy and cynical it seems to me now.

I must have been staring at my food too long because Patty called my name. "Owen, dear, I was just telling Attila here about your work and he's interested in hearing more about it."

Attila stared at me from across the table.

"It's not so exciting. We do the manuals for a large software company."

"Do you do all the layout as well, like the diagrams?"

"One of my colleagues does that. I'm mainly a text guy."

Attila waited for more. Patty joined another conversation. She had handed me off. Perhaps it was my mood, but the promise of the early part of the evening—the simple pleasure of watching my wife interact with others, even as I interacted with her—seemed all but crushed in this brief swerve of her attention away from me.

Letters started but never sent:

Mr. Raven,

I, too, am an upstanding individual, and I am pleased that you decided to reconsider your hasty ~~photo-based~~ assessment of my character. ~~You will discover soon enough that I am no mere dabbler in our correspondence.~~

~~Dear~~ Henry,

~~Have you ever felt utterly, utterly alone?~~ I have given your letter a great deal of thought, and ~~while my mind reels at the thousands of unexpressed expectations hovering out of reach (somewhere in the future)~~ I can safely and honestly cite what it is I want from you now. ~~Love is a difficult thing to summarize.~~ I am aware that ~~romance~~ ~~wooing~~ correspondence is a dance.

Sir:

It is crucial to start on honest footing ~~here.~~ I have never been one to stand on ceremony. I am eager to ~~move beyond these preliminaries and get on with our correspondence in earnest.~~ start. The story of my life could find a ~~resting place~~ home in your ~~receptive~~ warm heart.

Henry Joe,

I want someone to listen to me. <u>I want someone with whom I can share my ~~most~~ intimate moments. ~~I am not naive.~~</u> You are a captive audience; I want that, too. In exchange, I will be your ~~messenger reporter~~ eyes ~~from~~ to the world outside. And your captive audience, if you so desire. ~~Here on earth our punishment seeks us out eventually.~~

~~Yours?~~
~~Lily~~

9

It was one of those rare afternoons. Patty had gotten up early—3:00 p.m.—to run a series of errands before going off to work. I walked around the house, checked my email (spam), caught up on some bills. The phone did not ring. I sat down again with my work and shuffled words around, making middling progress. Later I lost my temper, throwing papers from my desk onto the floor, generally feeling angry at something indefinable and feeling sorry for myself.

I went to the bedroom—where on most days I would have found a Sleeping Beauty to comfort me—and face-planted onto the duvet. In so doing, I managed to eradicate from my senses all external stimuli but the feel of cool sheets and the sound of my own breathing. With this fetal isolation came just enough mental clarity to help me recognize why I had become so impatient: I was failing. I had barely begun and already I was failing. Patty was slipping away, and Raven's letter had been little more than a "What do you want from me?" I could take solace in the fact that he had written back, that some correspondence had been established, but was I any closer to my goal? My last drafts were no good. I hadn't sent anything out. They seemed so stilted. Where was any sense of femininity, of Lilyness, on that page? It was all *You ask what I want* and *I tell what I want.* Where was the seduction in that? Where was Lily's voice in all that Owen falsetto?

I had hatched a perfect plan and yet could not execute it. I was not going to give up easily. Lily would be more of a stretch than Lysander, but now I had one advantage: revision. No need to learn how to mimic surprise at a sound behind me. There were no sounds. Only words. I could rely on my strengths with Lily, I could research, then apply my findings. I could write and re-write my Lily until she was ready for Raven. By the time I rose from the bed I realized I had failed at only one thing: taking seriously the difficulty of my plan. Lily would have to be more than a computerized image, and she would have to be more than a set of cursory answers to Raven's questions. If he was going to fall in love with her, she would have to be lovable, seductive even, and the letters would have to seem not like some artificial and stiff charade of femininity, but like the by-product of a larger life.

I stood in the middle of our bedroom. The curtains were closed and the late afternoon sunshine had slipped under the hedge outside—the room was suffused with a dim orange glow. It was now a womb in which Lily was gestating. I pulled open the top drawer of the dresser in front of me. Folded and stacked in neat rows, Patty's panties—lacy or silky or cotton—sang a song of innocence and order, of cleanliness and intimacy. Compared to my boxers-and-socks drawer, Patty's underwear drawer was a museum display. I had pictured myself pawing through a mess of her underthings and pulling up from the bottom, by chance, the perfect pair of Lily-panties, but now I could see that pawing would never work—I would never be able to restore this kind of order. I brought my head closer and perused the sides of every stack, looking for a pair that seemed, upon visual inspection, both sufficiently elastic and sufficiently "Lily." I saw a candidate, stretchy-looking but feminine lavender, a bit older. It was the second from the bottom, and the stack to which it belonged had to be extracted carefully, as to not disturb adjacent stacks. I was not at the mall, after all, where some high school Sisyphus would come by after I was done destroying a perfectly folded pile of jeans to fold them all over again. I left the bottom pair of panties in the drawer (rotated fifteen degrees to mark my spot), dropped the ones I was after onto the top of the dresser, and lowered the remaining stack onto the "marker" pair, careful to maintain— as I had done long ago with my uncle's *Playboy* magazines— correct orientation so that Patty would not notice the stack had been disturbed.

The panties I had extracted were indeed lavender and indeed stretchy, but they also had a characteristic I was not expecting. They were thong panties. Reluctant to go digging around again lest I disturb my wife's perfect stacks, I settled on them anyway. I removed my pants and boxers and stepped into Patty's underwear. I threw my boxers in the hamper and pulled on my pants.

The last of the afternoon's light came through the trees and shimmered on the grass in that dappled way that reminded one of life's little miracles. (Nature uplifts. Cinderblock numbs.) I was no longer the failure I thought I was, even after I reentered my office to face the mess I'd made earlier. I left those papers on the floor and made my way straight to the desk. I had committed myself to being Lily for a while, so I decided to explore her. That evening I wrote something I can only describe as a fictional autobiography, an act of writing through which Lily would tell me about herself. I reproduce it here verbatim from memory.

My Life
by Lily Hazelton

My name is Lillian Echo Hazelton and I was born in Central California in 1970. My mother died in a hospital when I was very young and my father showed no interest in raising me, so before I even started school I came to Southern California to live with my mother's sister and her husband, who had a son a little older than I was. From then on my family life was stable in that we didn't move and no one died. But the sting of my early childhood in Central California never really left me. So I know what someone means when they say that trouble tends to follow them around. I am wearing a lavender thong. I live in a one-bedroom apartment, built in the 1950s and decorated by me. I like to cook but don't seem to do it that often. I have many acquaintances, a few of whom I would call close friends. I work at the local elementary school, as a teacher's aide, so I know children. I believe in a God but do not attend church, finding it too wrapped up in the affairs of man.

I had a short-term sexual relationship with my cousin when we were both in our teens. He was my first true love. Before love could be broken down into categories, we had the real thing together, the pure thing. But he was my cousin, and we were discovered, and now he is no longer with us. I am a liberal until threatened. Sometimes I forget to eat lunch. I rarely drink alcohol alone. I go months without masturbating and then diddle myself twice a day for a week. I want to know that you are not going away. When I'm in trouble, I call my aunt, who is difficult to talk to. When I need someone to talk to, I call my friend Francine, who despite her intense competitiveness usually provides a sympathetic ear. I have no one to talk to. My mouth moves, words come out, people nod and respond, but I never really get to talk to anyone. Since childhood, I have prayed for God to take my life. I have two cats and will not get a third because I do not want to be a single woman with three cats.

It was a thrill, creating her out of thin air, setting the trap for Raven. Life was going to be different soon. I was typing away under my desk lamp, the rest of the house dark, when I heard the familiar but unexpected creak and groan of the garage door. I looked at my watch and at my calendar. Tonight was a work

ANTOINE WILSON

night. Patty was supposed to go straight to work after running her errands.

I heard her footsteps in the hall, and then she appeared in the doorway with a peculiar look on her face.

"I'm ditching work tonight," she said.

I knew the look—the tight smile of a very responsible person doing something barely irresponsible—the shell of liberation. It was Patty's belief that if she were to act less responsible now and then, she would find herself to be a freer, happier person. But being irresponsible seemed to strain her and the consequences of her irresponsibility always came down on her as if totally unexpected. "Why do I always have to be the responsible one?" she would ask. "Other people get by just fine." She could never get used to the idea—she could never be convinced of it—that we irresponsible masses were constantly paying for our irresponsibility with additional heaping portions of stress, heartbreak, and bankruptcy. We did not lead the carefree lives she imagined for us.

She took in the disorder of my office.

"Jesus, Owen," she said. "What happened?"

Did she envy my devil-may-care attitude at that moment? She tiptoed across the archipelago of open carpet and pulled my head to her stomach.

"Are you finished for the day?" she asked.

"I could ditch, if that's what you mean."

"And if you did, what would you want to do tonight?" she asked.

"What do you want to do?"

"You," she said, "and Frisbee, and dinner."

66

"Three things that can happen in only one order." She looked disappointed for a moment, then went to the front closet and retrieved the Frisbee. Sex first would have meant no Frisbee, and dinner first would have meant no sex or Frisbee. Even in our limited experience we had learned this. Our sex life was a disaster. We went through great droughts punctuated with spasms of activity, based on how Patty was feeling. In the beginning, she would break down and cry during sex, claiming an overflow of emotion. CJ's ghost standing at the end of the bed.

It was one block to the park in the cool night. I walked as naturally as I could.

"You seem distracted," she said.

"I'm fine." The panties were a vice. When we got there we threw the Frisbee back and forth a few times. As was inevitable, it ended up on the ground. I couldn't bend to fetch it. I managed to flip it up with my foot, but could not get it high enough to retrieve it. I kicked it in a circle.

"Owen, what are you doing?"

I couldn't bear to look at her. I left the Frisbee on the grass.

"I should have gone to the bathroom before we left," I said.

"There's one over there."

The public restroom at the park consisted of a cute outbuilding—more handsomely appointed than the concrete hellholes down by the beach—and appeared very clean from the outside. I went in expecting the worst possible odors, graffiti-covered metal "mirrors," pooling fluids in the corners, but it was better maintained than I thought it would be, especially considering the half dozen or so homeless men who inhabited the park with their dogs, sleeping bags, malt liquor, and weed. The only thing I would have asked for, aside from a nice floormat, was a higher stall door. The city had equipped the toilets with thigh-high stall dividers and doors, just enough to provide a modicum of decency for the average sitting citizen while also not providing enough privacy for shooters to shoot, taggers to tag, lovers to love, or me to doff my wife's underwear in privacy.

I had removed my pants very carefully to avoid their touching the floor or the bottom of my shoes, and I had just slung said pants over my arm in order to pull off the panties when I heard a shuffling at the door. My first thought was Patty. The ball of guilt in my chest was being whacked back and forth by the twin paddles of justification and fear of discovery, and I had to remind myself that I was doing all of this for her, that she loved me, that I loved her, that I could explain everything and make everything okay again.

I was on the verge of explaining myself to the invader when I realized it wasn't her—it was a homeless man. We had seen him down at the corner coffee shop many times. He had a crew cut, a sharp square jaw, and his eyes were a tad too close together. He wore a military helmet from time to time and his cardboard sign usually read "please help $1 anything," though he seemed too able-bodied to be living on the streets and begging. He looked like a cartoon soldier, thus his sobriquet: the Cartoon GI. He spent most of his time—in residence at the coffee shop—drawing multicolored diagrams (with a four-color click-pen) of various worldwide conspiracies, with arrows joining a Union Jack to a (well-drawn) rat to the Stars and Stripes, with the words FLOW OF CAPITAL written over one of the arrows and U.N. GLOBAL P.O.W.

CAMP written over another. He posted these diagrams on telephone poles in the area. I used to collect them.

One evening I was dozing in the quiet cocoon of my home office when I heard yelling outside. Yelling was rare, a thing of the city. I went to the front door and poked my head out to see what was going on, and there he was, the Cartoon GI, making his way down the sidewalk with his helmet, his tightly rolled sleeping bag, his olive-drab pack. He screamed at random intervals, at the sidewalk ahead, although no one was there: "Niggers!" and "Mother fuck your nigger ass!" and so on, each phrase punctuated by the same racial epithet. Now I am sure there are white people in the world for whom the sound of that epithet means the safety and comfort of a redneck home, but for me it had the opposite effect—I understood, upon hearing the Cartoon GI screaming these words, that he was not as harmless as I thought he was. Ever since then, I had made a point of avoiding him, no longer peering over his shoulder to see what his latest diagram contained.

We locked eyes for a moment, he recognizing that I was standing in a pair of women's underwear, me recognizing him. He turned and walked out, cursing under his breath. I slipped out of the painful thong as quickly as possible and pulled on my pants, careful not to streak the insides with whatever was on the bottom of my shoes. The secret was to roll each pant leg into a donut and get the shoe through all at once. As for the panties, I didn't want to risk keeping them in my pocket. And I couldn't throw them away—I couldn't bear to imagine my wife's panties sitting atop a landfill somewhere. (Birds pecking at them.) There was a ledge at the top of the concrete wall, just under the roof.

By straddling the stall—standing on the too-low stall walls—I was able to reach up and tuck the panties there, under the eaves (but indoors) for safekeeping. I would get them in the morning. Mission accomplished, I hopped down and walked briskly—how free my parts felt!—out the door, almost bumping into the Cartoon GI, who'd been waiting outside for me to finish so he could go in.

There stood Patty, Frisbee in hand, eyes on me. I wanted to collapse at her feet. I have stolen something from you, sweetheart. I have deceived you. Sometimes I feel that nothing human is foreign to me, but at other times, I can be unsettled by the pettiest deception. Look at her. She stood before me and, relieved of the torture in my crotch, I could see her again. Why had I deceived her like this? I had to remind myself that all deception would fall away soon enough.

But what I really want to say is that the sight of her bony shoulders outlined in her black sweatshirt brought me back to something, which I wouldn't exactly call reality because I was already in reality, but which I might call context. Her unsmiling gaze made me feel like I had access to some former version of myself, one not tormented by those things currently tormenting me. She was a vision. Now she smiled. She handed me the Frisbee.

"That guy was scared of you for once," she said.

Ahh—that was the face she'd been wearing: the stored-up joke.

"What was going on in there?"

"Why? Did he say something?"

"Grumble, grumble, grumble." She imitated him, shaking her head.

"I guess he expected the place to himself."

I tossed her the Frisbee. We threw it back and forth a while, under the lights, in the drained concrete fish pond. The surface was smooth and even; it was like playing on a court. We did better than usual. The Frisbee made a horrible sound whenever it skidded along the concrete, so we played more cautiously than if we had been on grass. Her hair, which she'd pulled back in a ponytail, became a half-restrained mess, then a quarter-restrained mess; her limbs became limbs I wanted to wrap myself in. The wonderful thing was that I could simply look at her, watch her move. My wife.

When the Frisbee skidded to a stop somewhere between us, we both went to pick it up, and Patty said "Enough Frisbee," and we headed for the bedroom. There, she discovered that I wasn't wearing any underwear. Rather than asking why or commenting on it verbally, she hummed and smiled.

My underwearlessness reinforced the transgressions of her ditch day and she put her hands on the crown of my head in a not-so-subtle hint to drop to my knees. We fucked like we hadn't fucked in a long time. This was not the comfort of Owen and Patty making love. It was the animal thrill of two people fucking. The areas of my penis that had been chafed by the panties now felt extra-sensitive, raking in a sharper sort of pleasure, and despite my wanting to make it last forever, I came quickly. Life is like a dream, with alternating zones of clarity and obscurity.

I used to want to apologize: I'm sorry I fucked you. I meant to make love. I'm sorry I was transported like that. I see the error of my ways. Because I believed that sex was all about connection, consideration, communion, and all those other C words. I couldn't handle the reentry from fucking to love. Eventually I figured it out. Patty helped me understand that she wanted to fuck too, sometimes, wanted even to get fucked by me sometimes. We came down together: that was our communion.

She lay her head on my chest and looked up at me. This was one of the few angles from which, physiognomically, she didn't look sneering, snotty, or superior. She looked like an ingenuous and vulnerable young woman. I could only handle that look in small doses. Life takes ingenuous and vulnerable creatures and makes them suffer in ways they cannot understand, and then it snuffs them out.

"Let's open a little wine," she said.

She lit candles, too, and we ate dinner—"gourmet" mac-and-cheese, salad, Brussels sprouts—in the bathrobes my aunt and uncle had given us as wedding presents.

"This is the wrong wine for Brussels sprouts," she said.

"All wine is the wrong wine for Brussels sprouts." I laughed at my own joke and noticed that while she laughed, too, something was holding her back. I suspected the elation of ditch day had finally caught up with her, that her mind had begun, yet again, to reckon with consequences. I raised my glass.

"Here's to ditch day," I said. "A reminder to take a break from serious stuff once in a while."

"To ditch day," she said half-heartedly. She sipped her wine, then held up the glass again, eyes watching the guttering candle flame. "And . . ." She looked me in the eye now, as if steeling herself to make an admission. ". . . to CJ. Happy Birthday."

"Happy Birthday," I said.

My mind flashed to the look she'd given me in the doorway of my office, the Frisbee, the fucking: ditch day. Not a real ditch day, a true ditch day, but a ditch day with a purpose, a Stocking family holiday. I knew she had deliberated all evening about whether or not to tell me, that she had gotten caught up in my belief she was letting loose "for the hell of it," but in the end she had to tell me why she hadn't gone to work that night. She had to give me, the last person who wanted it, a good reason why she'd taken the night off.

10

The next morning a thick silver fog covered Our Little Hamlet by the Sea. Patty and I drove down to the local coffee shop. She seemed preoccupied by something, probably the hangover of ditch day, and I too was preoccupied, by the low-level but persistent fear that the Cartoon GI would emerge from behind some pillar and call me out. I couldn't get my mind off the panties. I was going to have to retrieve them soon. I was most concerned with what I was going to do with them. My latest ploy, after dismissing the possibility of just washing them (they would be stretched out), was to make it look as though the cats had pulled them from the drawer ("they were protruding, I guess") and stretched and damaged them in the course of their feline play, discovered by me too late to save the underwear from ruin. Far from foolproof, this plan seemed downright stupid in the light of day, thus my lingering anxiety, preventing me from being attentive to my wife.

"That was fun last night," I said.

"Yes it was." She spoke matter-of-factly, not disagreeing, but also not engaging me.

"Is something the matter?"

She placed her hand on mine, and I knew instantly it was nothing I had done. After a moment she spoke. "I was up really late last night. Couldn't sleep. I probably should have gone in to work or something. I don't know, that's not it exactly. It's always his birthday or a holiday or the week he died. I forget, you know, for a while, and then it all comes back the same as ever."

"Talking about it is healthy."

"Talking about it *is* healthy." She nodded. "But nothing changes."

"Nothing changes."

I moved my hand on top of hers. We sipped at our coffees.

"I need some sleep." She looked far away, then smiled. "Do you want me to drive you back?"

"I've got some errands to run down here. I think I'm going to hit the bookstore or something."

"In this fog? What if you get lost?" Her eyes sparkled. She seemed fine now. This was a remarkable capacity of hers—she could shrug things off by sheer force of will, could take something that was bothering her and force it not to bother her any more.

She went home, leaving me in the coffee shop parking lot, and I walked toward the park in the fog. The streets were humming with commuters, some of whom gave me questioning looks—why isn't *he* on the way to work? It's funny. When I was working at the office every day, our neighborhood didn't seem so full of 9-to-5ers, but once I began working more at home, walking the streets to stimulate my mind (a block for a block), I noticed how crowded the streets got when people left for work or returned home from it.

The park was deserted, save a few moms arriving at the playground near the north end of the park, pre-K kids in tow. I felt self-conscious walking alone in that park, as if a sign were flashing above my head (with a glowing nimbus, now, in the fog): PERVERT. I made my way to the restrooms and went in. Empty. I found my stall, which someone had defiled in the meanwhile, climbed up the stall walls, and reached my hand up to the ledge under the roof. Nothing but cool air coming in from outside— the roof was raised above the wall. I moved my hand from side to side. I couldn't actually see up there, but I could feel the entire thickness of the wall, to the outside edge, and the panties weren't there. I climbed down. I had picked the right stall, yes. I scanned the floor. Nothing resembling panties. I went outside, retrieved a stick from under a dying tree, and poked through the trash can inside the restroom. I managed to scatter paper towels all over the floor but found no underwear. Standing there in an ankle-high swamp of crumpled paper, I realized the underwear might have fallen off the wall to the other side. I experienced the epiphany of having found something mentally before going to confirm its location physically. I had obviously pushed the panties too far and they had gone all the way across the top of the wall, falling from the eaves on the outside of the building. I left the restroom and walked around the building to the back, where the shrubs pressed against the wall. I made my way to the corner below the men's room and pulled at the shrubs. Nothing up top. And, after I got on my hands and knees in the damp dirt, nothing under the shrubbery but old candy wrappers and a wax cup. The panties were gone.

At that time, I did not see those lost panties as harbingers of everything irretrievable. I was too wrapped up in the question of the moment: How would I explain to Patty what had happened? Walking home through thinning fog, I decided to play dumb about all of it. Patty might not even notice they were missing. And if she did, why would she suspect me of taking them? She wouldn't. This resolve gave rise to a secondary set of questions: Had someone taken the panties away? The custodians? Someone else? The Cartoon GI? And what if it was the Cartoon GI? Would he try to return them?

I was being haunted not only by the loss of the panties, but by the potential for that loss to reverse itself, like those dreams Patty and I had talked about, in which the dead come back to you as alive as they had ever been. The only thing I could do to distract myself from all of this was to write a completely new letter to Henry Raven. In that letter, I saw nascent glimmers of a woman on the page. As I recreate the letter now I find it hard to believe that these words—her words!—came into being as my fingers moved across the typewriter.

Dear Mr. Raven,

Thank you for the new picture—aren't you handsome in front of that red truck! As I mentioned, I had seen your picture before, on the D.O.C. website, so I knew you were handsome, in that noble warrior way of yours. But even though I had mentally "cleaned you up" dozens of times—you do look sleepy in that mug shot—I still had to take a second to catch my breath when I saw you in front of your truck, all newly-shaven and fresh-looking, and I knew I had made the right decision about following my intuition and writing to you in the first place.

I believe—and don't think I'm trying to convert you, because I am not a religious woman—that the universe communicates with us via signs and that we have to remain open to them at all times, or ignore them at our own peril. Fate, with a sign or two along the way, has led me to this moment, to me writing this letter, to YOU. I believe that, and I wonder what else fate has in store . . .

The other day, while I was still awaiting your letter, I sat drinking coffee on the landing of my apartment building. (It's more like a walkway for all the second story units, but there's enough room for a chair, and on a very clear day you can see a sliver of shimmering ocean on the horizon.) Some things had not been going my way at the school where I work—I'm a teacher's aide—and some people I thought I could trust turned out to be talking behind my back to the administration. People don't realize how political teachers can be. I don't want to bore you with the details, but I was in a miserable mood, and I thought some fresh air and coffee might help to boost my spirits. It didn't work. I sat out there and began thinking of all the bad things that could happen. It was like I couldn't stop my imagination from "going there." And one of the things I thought of was you. I confess I had begun to give up hope that you would write.

I tried to clear my mind and think about what I was going to cook myself for dinner (pork chops with applesauce, it turned out), and I found myself absentmindedly staring at the big maple tree beside my building. The wind was rippling the leaves and it was kind of pretty, so I kept my eyes on it for a second or two. Nothing I hadn't seen before, really, but it was like something said to me: "Stop, wait. Appreciate the moment." And so I watched the tree longer than I would have and you know what happened? A single leaf dropped. Just one. No leaves on the ground, mind you, and no others falling. I waited. No others fell. And I knew it was a sign, reminding me to appreciate my life. Just because one leaf falls, doesn't mean the whole tree does, too.

From that moment on, I didn't worry. I knew you were going to write back to me. And I knew that no matter what happened "out here" or "in there," we had already created a third place.

What if that red sun (it is almost down past the horizon now) was your red pick-up, coming to pick-ME-up?

Please write back as soon as possible.

Sincerely Yours,
Lily Hazelton

I waited four days to post Lily's letter. If writing it was like building a bomb, dropping it into the mailbox was like lighting the fuse. I waited for the explosion. With waiting came worry. How do people fall in love? I was pleased with the way she was coming out, as I learned to incorporate more of "the stuff of life" into what had been a generic woman. Still, I worried. Would Raven fall for my Lily, heart and soul? If he did not, if my plan fell flat here, Patty might drown in her sea of sorrow, or drift away from me forever . . .

I assuaged my worry the only way I knew how: research.

I went back to the GBS Books store near my house. I admit I was seized, upon entering the place, by an anxiety of influence. If I were to seek (and follow) outside advice in my seduction, would Lily seem less organic, more like a phony seductress out of some book? I have long known that the difference between good art and bad art is attention to detail. My Lily would have to be as complicated as any real woman, which was very complicated indeed. I would have to be vigilant, lest my research overwhelm me and turn Lily into nothing more than a paper doll. I ended up finding and buying three books—for under $20 total— in that moldy-smelling palace of words: *Literary Love Letters*, Horace Johnson, ed., a collection of love letters from various famous literary figures to their lovers; *The Greatest Love Poems of All Time*, no editor stated, with a gold-leaf cover and built-in pink satin bookmark; and *Seductress 101: How to Get and Keep a Man Using Your Inner Bitch*, by Susan Natches, MFCC, MSW, LCSW.

When I got home, I went immediately to my office and pawed through the books. I'd felt embarrassed to be looking through them at the bookstore, even though there was no one around. Something about Patty's coming home early on CJ's birthday had thrown me off guard—as if she could appear anywhere, at any time, to ask me what I was doing. I pictured her with the lavender panties hanging from her index finger. "Inner bitch, huh?" she would say. I felt much more comfortable at my desk, where I could bury the books in a drawer if she came home.

Literary Love Letters turned out to be all but useless. Who knew these so-called great writers could write such pap? There was obviously a difference between writing to your sweetheart and writing for publication. But it was useful in reminding me that Lily's letters didn't have to be perfect. They didn't have to flow like a well-organized software manual or business document. They had to overflow—with feeling. As far as lifting stuff from this book—no way. Most of it was antiquated, and belonged to lives other than Lily's. Copying someone else's love letter is like copying someone else's grocery list.

For a book containing a phenomenally concentrated base of human knowledge on the subject of love, *The Greatest Love Poems of All Time* looked as cheap and tacky as a Kleenex-box cover. Clearly, it had been slapped together by an editor looking to make a cheap killing off texts that had long been in the public domain. It contained many powerful lines and ideas. But I couldn't use them to seduce Raven. I realized, as I flipped past poem after poem by Virgil, Shakespeare, Petrarch, and others, that every one of these poems was meant to woo a woman. Who woos a man with poetry? Not Lily.

The *Seductress 101* book was full of practical tips, at least one of which I had already intuited in waiting four days to send my most recent letter. Unfortunately, most of the tips involved actually seeing the intended love object from time to time, so my dream of a turnkey step-by-step approach proved illusory. But Ms. Natches did provide some useful advice. By way of example, the following passage from her "Is He Interested?" chapter: "Oftentimes men will feign indifference toward their love interests. The less you let this affect you, the better. This is something men need to do in order to feel like men. The best way to get them to betray their feelings is by introducing another man into the picture. If your man gets jealous, he's interested." As I have mentioned, they will not let me have any of my papers, so that is entirely from memory. But I'm quite sure it stands exactly as written.

Lily would have to seem as alive as me or you if I wanted to have any chance of pulling this off. Every decision along the way would require increasing attention to consistency. I couldn't play at being Lily. The goal of a consistent Lily didn't seem insurmountable, except in one respect. Appearance. Raven would ask for more photographs.

He would ask for more photographs, sexier photographs, indoor, outdoor, everywhere photographs. The only photo he'd gotten already had been a one-off. I hadn't thought about having to replicate her over and over again. I can't even recall the number of steps I went through to put that first image together. To replicate that face (without simply cutting and pasting it) would have been like trying to replicate a Jackson Pollock. I thought of the pictures on the Stocking mantle, how different Patty looked from picture to picture, and yet they were all pictures of her. How would I be able to tap into a method for creating the appropriate amount of visual variety without making Lily seem like a dozen different people?

One evening, after I'd finished my day's work and before Patty had begun hers, we sat down to dinner as usual. Patty fidgeted with her utensils, moved food around her plate between bites. She was agitated, or so it seemed to me. Because of our off-kilter schedules, dinner was typically when flare-ups occurred. Patty, perky and well-rested, would commence one of her criticisms, and I would be too exhausted from a long day to defend myself properly.

"You've been working hard," Patty said.

"Hardly working," I replied.

She shook her head. "Why do you do that?" She brought a forkful of food to her mouth. "You downplay yourself long enough, you'll start to believe it." She chewed and challenged me to disagree.

"My mouth and my brain aren't that well connected."

"What are you talking about?"

"I think I can downplay myself as long as I want without believing it."

"I'm trying to have a substantive conversation, here."

"Me, too."

"When I say that you've been working hard, what I mean is that you seem sort of distant right now."

"Oh."

"I want to know what's going on inside your head."

"I want to know what's going on inside your head, too."

"Asulcena was here all day yesterday and she said you never left your office."

"I guess I was working."

"That's better."

"Making subconscious progress on user documentation."

Patty stood up to refill our drinks. "I don't know about her."

"Who?"

"Asulcena. She misplaces things. I wonder—and I feel bad saying this—but I wonder if she's taking things, too."

"What kind of things?"

She shook her head. "I shouldn't have brought it up. I'm thinking aloud."

"Okay. Everyone does it. But you let the monkey out of the bag."

"It's just that I couldn't find this pair of panties, and you know, they're only panties. But they were expensive. And now they've disappeared."

"Maybe they got folded into a shirt or something."

"I hate to be so paranoid, you know."

"Cautious, sweetheart," I said, "you're cautious. It's understandable."

Every future surprise party has its present misunderstandings, all of them to be resolved when the surprise arrives.

11

A few days later, Patty came home from work to find me packing a day bag. I told her that my aunt hadn't been feeling well, and that she'd been asking me to come by for a while. When Patty saw me packing the laptop, she asked why I was bringing it along. That's when I mentioned the research I wanted to do, into my family.

"I feel like it's time I knew my roots a little clearer," I said.

"You're bringing the scanner, too?"

"Sure," I said. "For old documents. Like family tree stuff."

"Fine, fine, fine." She planted on my face a passionless kiss.

Supportive Patty had turned into froward Patty. She didn't want to have sprung on her, as a surprise, that I might not be at home or at the office. She'd gotten used to keeping me in my place, to knowing always where I would be. As a means of managing her worry. People who have lost a loved one in sudden and tragic circumstances often exhibit this type of controlling behavior.

"I know you don't want me to go," I said, "but this is something I have to do, for myself. I promise I will be careful. I promise I will be here before you leave for work tonight."

"I would have liked advance notice on this one, Owen."

"Growth is never painless. You've got to deal with spontaneity. I know it's been hard, since CJ, to let go."

"This has nothing whatsoever to do with CJ."

"It's a perfectly normal reaction."

"This is not about CJ. Not everything is about CJ. This is about us. I just want to know ahead of time when you're going off on a six-hour round trip to go see your family. Besides, if you're so interested in your family tree, how come I haven't heard anything about it?"

"I've been trying to process certain things from my childhood. And I think I've found the solution in genealogy. So I need to make a short research trip. Is that so strange?"

"Genealogy."

"Yes."

"It's always something."

"What?"

"You always find some way to avoid life. Some pet project that's going to solve everything. But that's not how it works, Owen. This is life. You can't hide until it's all over."

"I couldn't agree more, which is why I'm going where I'm going right now."

"You also can't get out of things just by agreeing, Owen."

"I know," I said. "Give me time." I planted on her face a more passionate kiss, to which she acquiesced, and made my way out the door.

My aunt and uncle lived in a housing development, actually quite tasteful, as far as those things go. The variety of architectural styles and colors made it seem almost as if the neighborhood had sprung up organically, albeit with all the houses the same age. I was happy to see, upon my arrival, that neither of their cars was in front. My aunt kept the "two-car" garage packed full of boxes, with little pathways between the stacks. As a result, I could always tell who was or wasn't home by which car was or wasn't parked out front. Empty curb, no one home. I let myself in and set up my laptop in the den, next to the door that led into the garage.

I was raised by my aunt and uncle, and lived in the same house with them and my cousin Eileen starting at age eight. What happened was that my mother died when I was seven, and my father, with whom I am no longer in contact, was not capable of raising me. So my childhood was split in half. My father was interested in raising me himself and had every intention to do so. He was an honorable and loving man. Still is, probably. Overwhelmed with having to take care of a young boy and work at the same time, he had difficulty handling my mother's death. She died of cancer. She had been fighting it for five years, the majority of my life. My entire life with her seemed like a long preparation for saying goodbye.

She would go to the hospital for treatments, things would start looking up, she would come home for a while, make meatloaf—I eagerly anticipated her homecomings with meatloaf in mind—and return for more treatments months or even weeks later.

My last memory of her was in her hospital gown, standing at the window next to her bed, hooked up to an IV. I stood next to her. I had been looking out the window at the planes flying by—the hospital was near a small airport—and she had risen from her bed to stand next to me. I was afraid to look at her and did not turn around as she groaned with effort to leave her bed. Seeing my hands flat on the window, she put hers up next to mine.

"Never forget I loved you," she said.

"I won't," I said.

She said she felt faint. My father helped her into bed. I pulled my hands away from the window and watched as her handprints faded away while mine, greasy from a meatloaf sandwich, remained.

After she was gone, my father did his best to try to keep things together for me, but it was just too much. I was a temperamental kid, and I was always wandering in all directions, getting lost, finding myself in trouble. Other family members, my aunt in particular, wondered aloud whether I wouldn't be better off in a more stable environment. My father insisted on pressing forward, the two of us a family, "or bust." But my mother's death coincided with an increase in his workload, and I found myself alone for long stretches. Technically, he was home much of the time, but now that there were no more hospital visits, he dedicated more time to his inventions. His lab, which he'd set up in our garage, was strictly off-limits to me, containing as it did many dangerous chemicals. When he talked to me about his projects, he described the patents he hoped to receive, but in the end, he never invented anything worthy of a patent. I suppose he was something of a dreamer. My aunt, who had never wanted her sister to marry my father in the first place, took pleasure in describing his set-up as a drug lab, though I question the reliability of this view.

My mother's death affected me in ways I could not comprehend, and after I was arrested for shoplifting—the police had found me camping in an abandoned lot, tucked into a stolen sleeping bag—I was sent to live with my aunt and uncle. I spent the subsequent years, until college, at their house, in the company of my cousin Eileen, who initiated me when I was thirteen and she sixteen, as I explained earlier. My first love.

I should mention that the house I was visiting with the laptop and scanner was not the same house in which I had grown up. After Eileen died, my aunt and uncle sold that house and moved into this development, hours away from their old residence.

My aunt had moderate packrat tendencies coupled with a tremendous talent for organization. The garage was stuffed, but clean. She had taken Eileen's life and packed it into boxes as a museum worker might, so that it could be unpacked and reassembled somewhere else for exhibition. While she was doing this, neither my uncle nor I were permitted to touch Eileen's stuff or go into the garage. Once she was finished, we were again granted access to the garage, as long as we made sure to put everything back in its proper place. I was happy no one was home because I didn't want to have to declare my intentions to my aunt and uncle. As I said earlier, they avoided talking about Eileen in general, and bringing her up unnecessarily would reopen old wounds.

In the garage, I made my way through a corridor between boxes until I found the section with Eileen's things in it. Here was a life—a monument in dusty brown cardboard. I couldn't see the writing on my aunt's labels, so I pulled open the big garage door, flooding the space with light, with the sunny street, the green lawns, the children riding past on bicycles. Another world, never mind.

Adjacent to the boxes with Eileen's old books and art supplies I found what I was looking for. Two file boxes containing photo albums. Eileen and Friends. Eileen in Europe. Eileen '87. My aunt and uncle kept some photos in the house, but they didn't put them up on the mantel like the Stockings, and most photos ended up out here somewhere. I wanted later-Eileen photos, and those were in the albums she had compiled herself. I flipped through them, pulling out only those pictures with a large, clear image of Eileen's face, post–high school, and scanning them before replacing them in the album. She had always looked older than she was.

I worked like this for several hours, until I had amassed a solid cache of Eileens on my hard drive, then I put my computer and scanner away in my car. I sat on the sofa in the living room and waited for my aunt and uncle to come home.

My aunt was an extreme hypochondriac, and my uncle was a family physician. Their dynamic had been the same for the forty years they'd been together. She complained, he dismissed her complaints, she complained some more, in part about his dismissing her complaints, and he would then go through an involved process to demonstrate to her that her complaints had been groundless. He was proven wrong as often as she, yet the dynamic stayed the same. I tended to side with her, out of shared temperament, or fear—my mother had died of cancer, after all. My aunt's dire predictions seemed such a more accurate picture of life than my uncle's reassurances and dismissals of warning signs, real and imagined.

Eileen was the only one in the household who completely bought into her father's assurances. She coveted them, got hooked on them, solicited them from him. Every time she went out into the world, she saw that things were not going to be okay, and she ran home to her father, so he could contradict a world of evidence and reassure her as he had always done. These roles had been well established by the time I showed up. While I adapted to life with a new family fairly well for a child who had lost his mother and barely saw his father, I never felt as though I could squeeze myself into their little metaphysical universe. The sympathy I had for my aunt's complaints and worries was not strong enough to drag me into her camp, and my uncle's confidence in reason and his unremitting optimism never sat well with me, either, my life having provided plenty of evidence to the contrary. So I drifted between the poles of my aunt and uncle, and I fell in love with my cousin, in a way that made me want to be like my uncle. I wanted her to come to me for reassurance.

12

I read Raven's next letter standing in the Mailboxes Store. I remember it vividly because I felt the need to conceal my emotions (the fox, the horns, the chase!) from the other patrons in the store.

Miss Hazelton,

I wish I could say I lived with you in the "third place" you talk about. I look forward to your letters but life on the inside is ruled by routine. They don't want us to make our own place.

When you wrote about "a sliver of shimmering ocean" I thought it sounded nice.

My ex did not have a way with words like that. You don't want to hear about her but as I said before I am nothing if not honest. I can sense kindness in your letters. She used to harp on me all the time as if there was anything I could do about it.

Send a longer letter next time. I've got nothing else to do.

Kind Regards
Henry Joe Raven

The Mailboxes Store buzzed with activity. Just as I was coming to the end of the letter, I heard the mechanical bell of the front door and looked up to see who was coming in.

A young man stood in the doorway, wearing what appeared to be a brand-new shirt and tie. I smiled at this clean-shaven college grad, happy to have in my hand a letter from Raven, happy to share my good cheer. It was one of those miniature social interactions, and it would have been nothing more, I would have moved on, if the kid hadn't mistaken me for a Mailboxes Store employee.

"Excuse me," he said. He had papers in his hand.

"I don't work here," I said. He apologized and made his way toward the line at the counter. That was the end of our interaction. He left me wondering why he would mistake me for an employee of the Mailboxes Store. I had therefore become more alert to his presence. Otherwise I might have missed the following: when he got to the front of the line, he seemed equal parts nervous and baffled. The wife/sister behind the counter tried to look helpful but probably scared him all the more.

"Is this 3131 Extra Road?" he asked.

"Yes," she said.

"I'm looking for suite 1391."

The wife/sister nodded patiently. "That would be a PO box. Do you need to drop something off?"

"No," said the young man, "I was looking for a real person. Like in suite 1391. This is 3131 Extra Road?"

"That's what it says on the door. 1391 is a PO box. Sorry, kid."

He left, bewildered and disappointed. I must confess I felt a thrill at the boy's confusion, some schadenfreude, although only a moment before I had wanted to spread to him my good cheer. For I had already turned him into Raven in my mind, and was sampling the early fruit of what would one day be an enormous crop: when Lily, love of his life, would be revealed to him as a sham, a nonexistent suite-heart.

Dear Henry,

I'm sorry you had a bad week. I am sending a happy-looking picture in hopes of cheering you up. Why was your week bad? I know you might find it hard to write about sometimes, but I hope you will feel comfortable sharing that with me. And nobody can really <u>live</u> in the "third place," Henry—I meant that it's nice to have an outlet, someone to put a new perspective on things.

Things at the school have been exciting recently! The teacher I've been working with, Greta, recently underwent a surgical procedure, and as a result I've been teaching the class all by myself. As you can imagine, it has been exhausting. But I don't feel tired until the day is over. During the day, I move forward without a break, and I get so much energy from the kids. I feel like I want to fill their lives with good things, all the time.

The kids are in fourth grade, boys and girls, and they're at the age when they're just beginning to act like little men and women, thinking on their own, but still so dependent on the rest of us. I read to them, and we have extended discussions about what we're reading, lately about whether characters have treated each other unfairly. They're really into fairness, this group.

There is one boy, new to the school, who's having some difficulty joining the rest of the group. Whenever the end-of-recess bell rings, I find him at the edge of the playground, watching the clouds cross the horizon. He's sweet, but he tends to wander off on his own a lot, and I can't figure out if it's because he's more advanced or more behind than the rest of them. I suppose he's a bit of both.

I had put this letter down and am picking it back up now. I just put together a delicious-looking meatloaf (it is in the oven now). Breadcrumbs, ketchup, onions, peppers, ground beef (of course), cheddar, and a few other things, with bacon on top—an old Hazelton family secret. It is cooking up right now and filling the apartment with the most exquisite smells. Do they let us send you food? I would happily send you some. Or something else, if meatloaf is not to your taste.

You mentioned your ex. I don't mind you writing about her. As a matter of fact, I would like to know more about her, especially about why things did not work out between you two. (Your honesty, it goes without saying, is much appreciated.) As for me, I have not been with someone for a while. I was in a relationship that ended badly too. I won't talk your ear off (I mean write your ear off) about it, but let's just say that after him, I stopped dating. I needed time to decide what I wanted. Now I'm looking for someone upstanding, honest, decent, and of course handsome. Plus with a good sense of humor. And someone who knows how to treat a lady.

You said that I have a way with words. I think you do too. Does your facility have a good library? I could send you some books, if that's allowed.

Yours truly,

Lily

Enclosed with the letter was a picture of Lily smiling a broad smile, sitting at a teacher's desk, surrounded by children's drawings. Her hair was up in a ponytail and she looked both capable and youthful.

You have figured out by now where I got the new picture of Lily. As I mentioned before, trying to replicate her without cutting and pasting from Lily_1 had proven difficult and would only become more difficult with each successive request for a photo. I remembered how much Lily_1 had resembled my cousin

Eileen. Only a few hours from my home was a cache of images, a grouping of faces, looks, smiles, and frowns all belonging to one person who, with a few clicks of the mouse, could be made to look like Lily, and who could never be tracked down by looks alone, unless one were willing to follow her into the afterlife, and an afterlife existed, and one's looks were there preserved, and the veil of deceit was not permanently lifted at the moment of our dying.

I did not copy these images unmodified and send them off—I was not that crass. I couldn't make Eileen equal Lily, even if I wanted to. No, but I took Eileen's face and hair, and I put them on other women's bodies, digitally, and I colored her hair and accentuated her features in a regular way, so that I could replicate what I had done when the time came to make more images. I referred back to Lily_1, that happy accident of Photoshop collage, to make sure I was being faithful to my first image. I am no computer genius, and no visual artist. My first attempt involved a great deal of measuring. I felt like the phrenologists of yesteryear, measuring ratios of skull width to eye placement and distances between nose and chin as a function of the width of the nostrils. The more variables I discovered, the more ratios arose from those variables, and I found myself having to chart the whole thing out on a spreadsheet, so that the calculations wouldn't be too burdensome—and so they would remain trackable for future iterations.

I do not have the spreadsheet in my possession, obviously, though I could reproduce it here if it were required, and accurately so. By way of illustration: The distance, on the master image, between Lily_1's right earlobe and the left corner of her mouth was 51 mm. The top of her forehead was 85 mm from the center of her chin. Her eyes were 27 mm apart. I plotted twelve different points on Lily_1's face to digitize her features. When looked at alone, without an image superimposed on them, the plotted positions looked like a connect-the-dots drawing of a jet fighter, with earlobes for wing tips and chin as afterburner. It was hard to believe they actually marked the spots that made Lily_1 uniquely herself, but when Lily_1's image was brought to bear on the diagram again, the points matched up perfectly.

I have since discovered that people do this for a living, and do it better than I do. These so-called biometrics experts have broken up the human face into eighty "nodal points." My mere twelve points yielded sixty-six discrete distance measurements—imagine their spreadsheets.

I brought all this math to bear on an image of Eileen. The result was Lily_2. For the moment I convinced myself that she was a success, that Lily_1 and Lily_2 looked like two images of the same person. But the experience was like watching a film with the latest special effects, where everything looks "realistic" but not real, and even as you watch and believe, you know that ten years from now the images will look dated and computer-generated and corny, and you will wonder how you could have ever found them realistic. I was at a disadvantage here, because I had suspension of disbelief and Raven did not. If I were in his shoes, I would assume that Lily was sending only her "best" pictures, and so I would scrutinize them for some sense of what she "actually" looked like, in day-to-day life. I put Lily_2 away overnight, convinced but cautious.

When she emerged from the shadows of a well-disguised folder tree the next morning (. . ./ *typing_master/ tutorial/ images/ key_strokes/ Lily_2.jpg*), she looked like the victim of botched plastic surgery and—what's worse—did not in the least resemble Eileen or Lily_1. The numbers had failed. Or, I should say, my application of the numbers, my choice of the numbers, had failed, because if one were to throw pure numbers at the problem, she might have looked perfect.

My second approach was to clear my mind as much as possible and look again at Lily_1. Only after I'd assembled her had I connected her looks to Eileen's. I made a short list of subjective statements encapsulating how she both resembled and differed from the image of Eileen I held in my mind. Here is a sample (from memory, all from memory):

1. Lily's brow ridge looks like Eileen's, but her cheekbones are not as high or prominent.
2. Lily's nose bridge is like Eileen's, except a bit higher, and she has no cute cluster of freckles.
3. Lily's chin is pointy, unlike Eileen's.
4. Lily has brown eyes. Eileen's eyes are green.

Creating this list, I was overcome with a sense of uncanny familiarity—I had done this before. I had done this with Patty when I had started dating her. I remembered a particularly superficial moment (post–ski–trip) at which I picked apart her features for those that reminded me of my cousin, whom I still regarded as a paragon of beauty, and tried to find in Patty's face some shadow of my first love. I wanted to understand how Patty had so swiftly and completely rearranged my heart's loyalties. I was never able to get to the root of that mechanism. It remains a mystery.

I closed Lily_1 and opened an image of Eileen. I worked down my list, making changes one by one, and worked by instinct rather than by number, always keeping part of my focus on maintaining a natural look. I waited overnight again and examined Lily_2.2 in the morning.

She looked like a real woman, like Eileen but not like Eileen, both familiar and foreign. Promising. I crossed my fingers and loaded up Lily_1. Yes. It was her. Then I opened the first Lily_2, the one I had done by the numbers, dragged her out of the trash bin out of curiosity, to see how far I'd come, to give myself a pat on the back for succeeding the second time around. She was dull, out of proportion, lifeless. I wanted to condemn the numbers but I couldn't. Some part of me had decided what to measure and how to define it.

The remarkable thing was, her features weren't too far off. Now that I could examine her free from anxiety, I saw not a badly reconstructed face, nor a decade old special effect, but something else altogether: a tell-tale dullness. Opaque as a candle. In contrast, the skin of Lily_2.2 maintained the brightness of Eileen's skin from the original photograph—I had restored it, from Lily_2 to Lily_2.2, from opacity to translucency, from dull reflection to bright glow, from death to life.

13

I heard Patty in the living room. She'd been home from work for a little while. Those simple routines—what I would give to have them back. The morning, her arrival, her "dinner," my breakfast, the peaceful day ahead, a trip to the office, the Mailboxes Store. I found her crumpled on the sofa, embracing a carton of wheat thins, watching a video of CJ and his friends.

They walked down to a local playground and took turns filming each other hanging upside-down from the monkey bars, camera inverted so that everything looked right-side-up. Aside from unruly clothes, hair standing on end, and increasingly reddening faces, the illusion was successful. One of them spat. The spit went straight up. Objects flew toward the "sky." And every time something flew up instead of down, CJ and his friends telegraphed their surprise with exaggerated expressions.

I grabbed a breakfast bar and left Patty laughing on the couch, tears streaming down her face.

Lily:

My ex was a bitch cunt whore from outer space. She
was a bitch because of the cruel way she abused my
feelings. She was a cunt because she made me feel like
everything was my fault which it wasn't. She was a
whore because she was running around out there while
her man was in here. She was from outer space because
no fucking human being would abandon another human
being like she did in his greatest moment of need. Anyway if you can't handle that Miss Teacher tough shit
for me huh? I am just sick and tired of everyone in this
world not keeping up their end of the bargain and me
taking the rap all the time.

Raven

The upside-down CJ video brought with it a whole new
period of crying. One would think he had died the week before.
Patty took several personal days off work, watched the tapes in
rotation. I tried to comfort her as best I could. My efforts had
no effect. Somehow we had gone backward in time. My mission
became more urgent than ever. I do not have a great imagination. Lily was stirred to life using what pieces I had. From
Minerva's story, to my mother's meatloaf, to a con-man episode
of *Wanted: America*. We are all bric-a-brac, odds and ends, I have
said this somewhere, but Lily would have to contain much more
of the personal ingredient if she was going to successfully draw
Raven into her clutches. I would have to don the heart's armor.

Mr. Raven,

Thank you for sharing your feelings. I suppose I should begin to expect a spirited tone from you now and then, particularly on the subject of your ex. She must have really hurt you. My ex really hurt me too. It took me a long time to get over it. I don't say "get over him" because I got over him more quickly than I got over the psychological wounds he left behind. Basically, we were together for two years, about to get engaged, and things were going great. We went out to a lot of romantic dinners and stuff, and he kept encouraging me to move in with him. But, thank God, I didn't.

He was not who he appeared to be.

I found out one day when I decided to surprise him at work. I knew he worked in a large downtown law firm, so I went to their headquarters and asked for him. They couldn't find him in the directory, so they sent me to someone else who worked for the firm. That person told me that my ex hadn't worked there for three years, and that he wasn't a lawyer at all, but a legal proofreader. It took some digging, but I found out more, and I discovered eventually that he had a number of aliases, and that he was wanted for scamming several young women out of their money.

He had targeted me. I had never told him about my money (I have some savings, thanks to my father's inventions) and yet he knew that I was a good target. I'm not sure what he would have done with my money, but apparently he'd been doing this a long time. I found out that he'd been looking through my files and I confronted him about it. The next day he disappeared completely. Without a trace. No phone call, no note. And nothing since.

The police said I was lucky—he didn't get the chance to rip me off. I say I was ripped off plenty—in the heart region. I don't know how he was able to simulate his love for me. It is so baffling I can't help but think he really did love me, even though I know he was really scamming me. It was horrible.

Maybe that's why I decided to write to you in the first place. You're not going anywhere. I will send more pictures when you write me a decent, polite letter.

Yours truly,
Lily

Dear Miss Hazelton

I got to thinking about my ex because you had asked about her in the letter before and I got so pissed off and I felt like I was writing to her instead of you and I'm real sorry.

Your story about your ex is sad but I won't pretend I haven't heard it before. Lots of men roam this country looking to prey on young women of means such as yourself and some of them end up living at my current address. Give me the name of your ex and I will be happy to take care of him if I ever see him anywhere. You are a nice girl I know that already it is obvious and anyone who does that to a nice girl deserves to pay.

It makes me think of your students and their sense of fairness. What happens to that when we grow up? I'll tell you. The system tries to make everything fair for everyone supposedly. (Tell that to the blacks.) You do something bad you go to jail you learn your lesson. That's the fairy tale. Nobody in here is learning about fairness. Everything that happens to you in here reminds you that the world is unfair. Who should be surprised that people don't play by the rules when they get out? I've got a lot of ideas about life. I'm not just some criminal. But I meant to talk about your kids. What if you could sic your kids on your ex? I bet a large group of kids could tear apart an adult man easy. That would be fair.

No religious books.

I keep picturing my arm around your waist. I remember being on the outside putting my arm around my girl's waist and not thinking a thing about it. Now I would give up my right ear.

Send me another picture. Nothing naked—they don't allow us porn here and it will get confiscated and end up in some guard's collection.

Yours too

HJR

14

"Neil, I can hear you breathing."

"Huh? I'm eating."

"I can hear you breathing all the way over here in my cubicle. Would you please stop?"

"I can't stop breathing."

"Can you stop eating?"

Neil appeared behind me. I could see his reflection in my computer monitor. I did not turn around.

"You okay?" he asked.

"I'm fine."

"'Are you writing a letter?'" He did a pirouette.

I shut off my monitor.

"You know," he said, "like the graphical paperclip that comes out to help you?"

Now I turned to look at him.

"Why are you bothering me?" I asked.

"Why are you in such a bad mood?"

Despite his being annoying, Neil was one of the few people I could talk to about my personal life. It was a consistent complaint of Patty's that I failed to cultivate and retain new friends. I was of the opinion that my old friends were plenty, despite their being dispersed across state and country. I could not see the point of starting up a bunch of new friendships. Patty was better at it, anyway, and not only in drumming up new prospects but in judging the respective character of said prospects.

Back when I tried to start new friendships, I would usually pick someone not to Patty's liking, she would warn me about them, I would ignore her warning, and the friendship would go up in flames within a short period, Patty saying "I told you so" without ever uttering those exact words. So when I needed to talk to someone, I talked to no one, or to Neil.

"Patty's having a stressful week, and it's overflowing onto me, I think."

"She still dealing with her brother?"

"She's hit a bad stretch again."

"Yeah," he said, "that's rough. We've had a pretty crappy week ourselves. Geraldine hit an opossum with her car the other night, and the kids have been crying about it ever since. It's amazing how something like that can affect people."

"Dirty little animals," I said, "and stupid—running into the street like that."

Dear Henry,

Your arm is around my waist. I can't believe I just wrote that. But I did, so I'm going to let it stand. That's not even first base, is it? I hope I'm not being forward. I look at your letters and think, no, of course I'm not, and then I go through my day and doubt creeps in until I am with your letters again. Still, I'm not exactly sure where we stand, and I'm not sure I want to know—maybe that's part of the excitement?

You're right about the system, I think, and its lack of fairness. If the system was fair, my ex would be caught and locked up. The heart is not fair either, I think, because in spite of everything he planned on doing to me, I would still feel bad for him if he ended up in prison—I can't erase that last bit of sympathy for him. I kept waiting for him to show up and explain himself. But hearts and systems aside, we all get punished somehow, don't you think? I don't mean in "the afterlife"—whatever that means. Here on earth our punishment seeks us out eventually.

I've decided that each of my letters should contain some news of the world out here, so that you can share part of my daily life with me. Will you try to do the same? I am curious about what you do with your days and nights.

Greta's condition turned out to be worse than the doctors thought, and she required some more surgery, which turned out to be major. The district has hired a proper substitute, a fellow named Clancy something-or-other who wants all of the kids to call him Mr. Clancy and asks the same of me. He is young and incompetent and so I am the teacher de facto. The only thing endearing about him is the fact that he wears tweed jackets with elbow patches, like an old-fashioned professor. And I suppose he is quite smart, but at this level street smarts are more important than book smarts, and he's awfully stiff, and the kids do impressions of him behind his back. He usually ends up sitting behind my old desk grading papers and twirling his moustache—though not in a movie-villain kind of way, more like an absent-minded professor. I'm not sure, but I think "Mr. Clancy" might be developing something of a crush on me. I do not intend to encourage him.

I will send you a picture with my next letter. In the meanwhile, here's a book for you to enjoy (and employ?): *The Greatest Love Poems of All Time.*

Yours,

Lily

PS I saw the saddest sight this morning. I went on an early walk, to get the blood flowing. Just down my street, in the middle of the road, was an opossum someone had hit with their car. From a certain angle, he looked like he was sleeping peacefully in the road. He had the sweetest little face. But when you walked around him you could see that his skin was broken and that his innards had spilled onto the asphalt. I just wanted to cry. I still want to cry. I told someone at work about him and they dismissed me, saying that opossums were ugly and stupid. I can't help but get torn up about all the little animals, Henry. They're all dying, all the time. I don't mean to be morbid, but the world is not a fair place. I am just thankful that I have you, and that you are not going anywhere.

Henry—

Did you get my last letter? The book? I haven't heard from you in a while. I hope I wasn't too forward. Here is a picture to remind you to write.

Lily

Dear Lily

The picture is hot. The reason I didn't write was because I was in the hole and they don't let us write in there. I ended up in the hole soon after I got your first letter so there was no time to write back before I got locked up for fighting with another inmate this shithead named Stewart who was trying to put his hands on your picture. The hole is a crap place to be especially for eight days. It would have only been four but I told them the truth when they asked and said I would have killed him if given another chance. So I got four more days for telling the truth. You can see what kind of values count in here.

I'm in a counseling program because it's a good idea if you want to get out. The more you bang your skull against the walls the longer they keep you in here. Mainly I tell them what they want to hear but after being in the hole eight days I was wiped out and I told the counselor about you. She said it was good for me to share my feelings with someone. She said not to get my hopes up too high. Remember what happened with my ex. If I wasn't so good at controlling myself I would have ended up in the hole for another month right there for squeezing her neck. But I did a countdown and cooldown.

Those eight days were tough. I was slipping in and out of dreams by the end. Here was one: I was punching Stewart over and over. Everyone was around me cheering and the more times I punched him in the face the stranger he started to look. I punched. His face looked younger. I punched. He had glasses on. I punched. He sprouted a moustache. I punched. He fell to the ground wearing a jacket with elbow patches. Do you recognize "Mr. Clancy"? The mind is a funny thing especially in the hole.

Yours
Henry

15

I should mention here that I have made a painstaking effort to ensure that every one of these letters is accurate to the word. Thanks to both the intensity of the communication between Lily and Raven, and to the sparseness of my current surroundings, I have been able to transcribe these letters entirely from memory. This is because I had to "become" Lily when I wrote, and even more so when I read. In the unlikely event that I have memory trouble, all I have to do is shift my mind over one mental notch, as it were, and everything comes back clearly.

Dear Henry,

Sounds like it was a difficult time for both of us. I was in a bit of a "hole" myself, as Greta's condition turned for the worse. She had been having minor digestive problems at first, and they got really bad. Up till then, she thought she was just like anyone else. Turns out she was bleeding internally, from ulcers or something, and they had to operate on her. Well, once the doctors got in there, they saw she had colon cancer, which people tend to think of as a man's disease for some reason. They took her colon out, and now she's going to have to wear a bag for the rest of her life, which is horrifying enough, but what's worse is that the fight is not over. She's going through a course of chemo and radiation treatments. It's awful. The kids (with my encouragement) made her a giant Get Well card. I went to see her at the hospital the other day. She looked physically weak, but emotionally strong. Pale and puffy but smiling, and with those eyes that could always shut down students who were horsing around. The spirit was still there. When she saw the card, though, she just wept and wept. There is nothing more horrible than watching a good, innocent person like Greta endure such senseless suffering.

The secondary upshot of this is that I haven't been able to get rid of Mr. Clancy just yet. He's developed a rapport with some of the kids now, and it turns out he's got quite a sense of humor. (Very, very dry.) He's been on-and-off touchy-feely since Greta went into chemo. He doesn't seem to know how to act around me. I feel like he wants to be sympathetic but doesn't know how. Or he's playing hard to get. Don't you wish that people, instead of being people, could just broadcast their intentions all the time, through a sign on their foreheads? Life would be a lot simpler then, and probably more honest.

I drove down to the beach after school the other day, to collect my thoughts. It was one of those blue-sky days when the clouds are all bunched up over the ocean, as if waiting to come to shore after the sun goes down. The breeze was surprisingly chilly—I always forget how cold the beach can be—but I took my shoes off and walked in the sand for a while. How I wish I could share with you the feeling of freedom I experienced! There is nothing like a walk on the beach to recharge your spirits. I wonder if I could describe it to you well enough someday that you might feel you were actually there? I know we haven't been writing each other for too long, but I must express how happy I am to have someone to share my feelings with. Sometimes I feel cooped up inside my own head. If it wasn't for you, I wouldn't have any release valve at all.

Write back soon!

Yours,
Lily

Lily

I got some time to look at the poetry book you sent and I have enjoyed it. At first the poems seemed like they were full of strange language. I'm not stupid but I don't know a lot of old words. I spent some time going back and forth to the library here (yes there is one but the books are not good) to look at the dictionary. After a while I got the hang of it. I think it was more me getting in the way than the poems being hard. These poets had some serious feelings. Some of the poems are funny like when a guy is trying to convince his girl to go to bed with him. Some of them are too show-off. There's a few supposedly written from prison but I think they're bullshitting. My favorite ones are the ones that make me feel like the poem is mirroring my thoughts if that makes any sense at all.

For example I read "A Dream Within A Dream" because the title reminded me of being in the hole and the poet (Edgar Allan Poe) was someone I have heard of before. Well it turns out the poem is about how I'm feeling right now. So maybe I'll stop writing and let Mr. Poe do the talking:

> Take this kiss upon the brow!
> And, in parting from you now,
> Thus much let me avow—
> You are not wrong, who deem
> That my days have been a dream;
> Yet if hope has flown away
> In a night, or in a day,
> In a vision, or in none,
> Is it therefore the less gone?
> All that we see or seem
> Is but a dream within a dream.

I stand amid the roar
Of a surf-tormented shore,
And I hold within my hand
Grains of the golden sand—
How few! yet how they creep
Through my fingers to the deep,
While I weep—while I weep!
O God! can I not grasp
Them with a tighter clasp?
O God! can I not save
One from the pitiless wave?
Is all that we see or seem
But a dream within a dream?

Sincerely
Henry

PS I was wondering what kinds of things your father invented.

Dear Henry,

Well, I am flattered that you've sent me a poem already. You must have noticed that the poem starts with a kiss! Are you trying to woo me? It's funny, every time I write something like that, I feel good, sort of liberated, then afraid—I think it's because I can't see your reaction right away—I usually feel relieved only after I receive your letters. Anyway, good to hear you're delving into the poems.

My father invented a variety of interesting things. He was a chemist. He developed some new kinds of plastic, when he was still fairly young, and received patents for them. The licensing fees for them still feed into the estate. I did not grow up with him, being raised by my aunt and uncle mainly, but this was a matter of necessity rather than neglect. I think he hoped to make it all up to me by leaving behind a fortune. Basically, he wasn't around much when I was growing up, and by the time he became rich, I'd gotten used to life without him. The funny thing is, I would much rather have had him around back then than have this small fortune in the bank now. Money or no money, I would still be doing the same thing. The kids are my passion.

Which brings me to the subject I've been avoiding for a whole page now. Mr. Clancy has announced to me, in his stiff way, that after Greta returns (it should be a matter of weeks if all goes well), he would like to ask me out for dinner. He said he wouldn't think of doing so while we are still colleagues, but wanted to let me know that I had piqued his interest, as he put it. Now that puts me in a dilemma. Because he is a sweet man, and he seems to enjoy many of the same things I do, such as the children, and reading, and I don't feel quite as repulsed by him as I did initially. But I cannot pretend like you and I have not been engaged in some old-fashioned courting ourselves. Or haven't we?

Please, please know that I will always be honest with you. The last thing I want to do is lead anyone on.

I know he's out here and you're in there, and that you've had to deal with that as a factor in the past—or at least you've implied as much—in dealing with your ex. You must understand, though, that it does not make a difference to me. After all, my ex was out here and he ended up being no good. I would much rather have a fulfilling relationship with an incarcerated man than a bad relationship with a man on the outside.

This letter seems awfully garbled now that I reread it. Let me put it to you as clearly as I can: If I had a sign on my forehead, it would say: "Should I tell Mr. Clancy to go away?"

(I have an answer in mind, but I'd like to hear it from you.)

Sincerely,
Lily

Dear Lily Hazelton,

I am writing to you on behalf of my cellmate Henry Joe Raven. He is in disciplinary hold at this time, and will not be able to write for a few days. He asked me to pass on this message to you: IF YOU WANT ANY MORE LETTERS FROM ME TELL CLANCY TO GET LOST.

Thank you,
Moses Lundy

Never forget, Raven, that I had you in hysterics, in and out of disciplinary hold, over my fancy Clancy. Never forget the anticipation in the pit of your gut when you heard the mail call. How many nights did you fall asleep thinking about your sweet Miss Hazelton? How many chambers of your honeycombed heart did she illuminate with her sweet light? And her photographs, smudged with grime and rubbed away at the edges—how many nights did you spend with them, with that sweet 4 x 6 world, that other dimension, populated by anonymous figures and the long-gone shade of a true innocent? Raven, when you pulled that trigger, was there a real human being in front of you? Or had someone wandered onto your game board? The pawn you took was someone's child and brother. Maybe you knew that. Maybe you didn't care. But your game board, it turns out, lies atop someone else's, and you don't know the rules.

16

Out of the blue, Patty suggested we go "on a date," like we used to do.

"I need to get out of the house," she said. "Besides, it's starting to affect you, working so hard."

"I'm getting stuff done," I replied, even though I was getting nothing done at all. The stack of pages in my desk now consisted of letters to and from Raven, various notes taken on the subject of love, and modified photographs. Those documents were nothing but the contrails of a process, the receipts from a surprise party, nothing in and of themselves but the side-effect of my plan. Not to be shared with anyone, except Patty, and only then when I could provide proof that her brother's murder had been properly avenged.

She suggested the pier, to which neither of us had been in over a decade. She had recently read an article in one of her lifestyle magazines about revisiting the wonders of childhood places. Whereas a more poetic-minded individual might flip through photo albums or ask her mother to corroborate fuzzy memories, Patty embraced her scientific literal-mindedness and decided we should revisit the pier in person. The amusement park from Patty's childhood had been destroyed in a storm, but a new version had recently been erected.

"Sure," I said, "why not?"

"You could try to sound at least a little excited."

"No, no. I am excited. I was just finishing up a few things in here."

She went to the bedroom to get dressed, while I put away some of the Lily stuff I was working on. When she reappeared, she was not wearing black anymore. She wasn't dressed up for a fancy night out or anything; she had put on a light orange sweater and some khaki pants.

"You're not wearing black," I said.

"I was getting tired of it," she said.

"Tired?"

"I opened the closet, and there was a huge row of black clothes. I saw some color, hiding in the corner, and I decided to put it on. Before my closet went black all the way across."

"Jesus, Patty. This is a big deal."

"Let's just go on a date, okay?"

"To the pier."

"To the pier."

We got in the car and drove toward the ocean.

"Remember," she said, "the Beach Rider and the Bump-a-Dump? Those were my favorites."

I had only been to the pier in its post-destroyed, pre-rebuilt stage, under very different circumstances. "I remember Eileen buying weed from a cholo on a big tricycle. It was laced with PCP. We were high for eight hours."

"You know what I loved? Those giant clouds of cotton candy."

"I remember a cloud of flies. Couldn't figure out if the guy was dead or asleep."

"You could watch the sunset from the Ferris wheel."

"Pieces of that wrecked Ferris wheel used to stick out of the water and skewer surfers."

"I remember. CJ used to surf there. My mom was worried sick about him."

All roads lead to CJ. We were quiet for a while. We drove under the neon arch at the entrance, down the steep ramp toward the parking lot. I paid seven dollars for the privilege of parking on the pier itself.

Our car rolled bumpily over the wooden surface of the disappointed bridge. That's from some other book, something I read in college. I got the joke, thought it clever at the time, but somehow looking at this pier, at the blue glow of the Ferris wheel against the red sky, I got the sense that the pier was quite satisfied with its carny feel, with its rides, its garish curlicues, its lack of utility—boats no longer pulled up to it—and that the bridge, that workaday structure, bearing nothing but traffic all day, might even find itself jealous of the pier, despite the latter's not reaching an "other side." A pier is a liberated bridge.

We walked hand in hand to the main section of the pier, through crowds of people bunched in groups of two or four, or clumped around vendors, such as the white-bearded man who could write your name on a grain of rice, the red-bereted caricaturist, the dumpy frizz-haired woman hawking watercolors of the sea, and so on. The sense in the air was not urgency (where could we go anyway?), nor was it total relaxation—the pier was too crowded for a leisurely stroll. More like a pleasant sea of potential threats—after all, this was where the poor kids could congregate for free, and gangs were always a presence.

Among the potential threats, Patty's cavalier attitude toward trading her mourning black for khaki and orange. She looked like the Patty of old, the pre-murder Patty. The transformation had been as simple as pulling clothes from a different part of her closet. Yet the transformation was not complete. Patty was the same woman she had been yesterday, as likely as ever to get tangled up in memories of CJ. Did she believe she had changed, or was her sartorial switcheroo an attempt to change herself from the outside in? Either way, this impulsive behavior was not the way she typically did things. I worried she might try to jump into the ocean.

Patty stopped short.

Someone almost bumped into her and said, "Hey—watch it."

"Why'd you stop?" I asked Patty.

She crouched down and placed her palms on the wood. "Feel this."

I did the same. "What?"

"Wait."

I waited. Nothing. Then a rumble, a bump, and a shiver. People walked past us now without taking note—we'd become an instant fixture. Rumble again, bump, shiver.

"The waves are breaking right here," she said. "That's the 'bump.' They're standing up and hitting the pilings directly below us. We're on the spot. It moves around, depending on the tides." She was thinking aloud. "And people are walking by like it's nothing. There should be a marker—one that moves—to tell you where this spot is."

"They'd have to pay someone to move it back and forth."

"No, but isn't this—" Rumble, bump, shiver. "Isn't this beautiful?"

I stood. "Why don't we go to the railing, where we can actually watch it happen?"

"In a minute."

I walked to the railing. She remained there, crouched down, palms flat on the ground, the flow of pedestrians opening and closing around her. In an orange sweater and khakis. Her eyes were focused on nothing, moving back and forth, like she was reading Braille. I turned toward the water to watch the waves hit the pilings. A seagull sidestepped on the rail and took flight. The waves checked the pilings, then passed right through them, again and again. Marching across the sea to arrive there, stand up, fall on their swords, and vanish eternally. A pair of arms wrapped themselves around my waist.

She kissed my neck. "You know what amazes me about all this? The waves never stop. They keep going without a break, sloshing around, like forever. These waves were pounding the shore before man ever walked the earth. That's astounding."

The seagull returned to the railing and pointed one beady eye at us.

"You could say the same for a lot of stuff," I said. "Volcanoes, for example."

Patty unwrapped her arms from my waist and sidled up next to me on the railing. She focused her gaze on the beach. "You contradict me a lot, you know that?"

"No I don't."

"Seriously. I'm trying to be positive here. I'm trying to steer things toward the good stuff. For both of us. And you persist in undermining me."

"Do you want to go on the Ferris wheel?" This was an olive branch. I hated the Ferris wheel, she loved it.

"Are you even aware of what you're doing, Owen?"

"I'm suggesting we ride the Ferris wheel."

"I was trying to talk to you."

"Do you want to ride the Ferris wheel or not?"

"Of course I do. I'm trying to say, though, that I've noticed a change in you. I wanted to get you out of the house. Spend some time together. Actually talk." She sighed. "I know things have been difficult. But I feel like you're not as curious about me as you used to be."

"That's bullshit," I said. I stopped and thought for a moment. "I'll always be curious about you, Patty. You're complex."

"I'll take that as a compliment."

"You should. I've just been more internal recently. It's an occupational hazard." She leaned into me. "Don't worry," I said, "I will make it all up to you."

I felt horrible. I'd put out the fire, but reassurance was a dangerous game, emotionally. I wasn't sure if I believed everything I had said. Except of course when I said I'd make it up to her. What else had I been doing? I needed to get back on track.

All those pictures of Eileen had temporarily interfered with my otherwise stable feelings for Patty. While I was scanning images, going through old memories, I could feel my heart drifting off course. But I knew it was temporary. Hearts drifted and found their way back to port all the time. When the Ferris wheel put us at the top and stopped, Patty insisted on standing to better enjoy the view. I asked her to please sit down. She sat and took my hands in hers. The basket swiveled in the breeze. Once everyone had gotten on, the rickety contraption began its rotation in earnest. My hands never left Patty's. Round and round we went, each rotation punctuated by the reappearance of the red-faced operator on his platform, his sinister smile directed at passing riders. When they let us off, I ran to the pier's railing—out of sight, behind the rides—and threw up.

"I must have eaten something funny," I said. "My stomach was feeling bad beforehand."

She rubbed the small of my back. "You poor thing. Why didn't you say so?"

"Didn't know I was going to throw up."

I felt the relief of one who has thrown up. We hunted around the concessions for someone who would sell us water. I swished it around in my mouth and spat it out over the railing.

"You want to walk to the end? Breeze might help refresh you."

"Sure," I said.

We joined the flow of couples meandering to the end of the pier, where there were no amusements or concessions, only a city-owned building, closed to the public, and a smattering of subsistence fishermen packing up the day's catches. The sun had gone down just before we rode the Ferris wheel, so the sky had gone from reddish to indigo, and the moon had spread its silver carpet on the rippled ocean surface. A moonglade looks so much like a path across the water, and it always points at you—how can you help but feel elevated by it? We took a moment at the end of the pier to stare into each other's eyes.

"Do I have puke breath?" I asked.

"Nope."

She kissed me. We kissed. We were not the only couple standing at the end of the pier kissing, but it seemed like we were. She had been right to insist on a date night. I could already feel the big wooden captain's wheel turning as my heart found its proper bearing again.

On the walk out to the end, I had absent-mindedly scanned the people sitting on benches or leaning against the railing, in sort of a baseline threat-assessment of all loiterers. One couldn't be too careful on the pier, especially with someone as blissfully oblivious as Patty (her child's image of the place overlaying the more complicated and treacherous reality). However, I had failed to notice a particular somebody encamped next to one of the benches, panhandling.

It was the Cartoon GI. I tried to guide Patty to the other side of the pier as we headed back, but she stayed her course, thinking I was playing a walking game with her. I tried to keep my head down, hoping he would not notice us, praying he wouldn't recognize me. Patty, unfortunately, recognized him first.

I handed him a five-dollar bill, concealing it so Patty couldn't see how much I'd given him. He stared at me coldly when he took the money. We walked away, Patty leading. I looked back for an instant, to make sure he wasn't going to talk to us or follow us, and I saw him hunched over his bag, rifling through its contents. He was pulling things out now, at a furious pace, making a pile out of his belongings next to his bag. It was difficult to see what he was trying to accomplish. Maybe he was going to put the fiver deep into his bag? The last thing I saw him pull out was a small balled-up piece of purplish cloth. The lavender panties. I was certain of it. My mouth went dry. I turned away, noticed that the Ferris wheel lights had cast everything in a pale blue. It could have been anything. My mind was playing tricks on me. I kept my hand at Patty's waist, kept her moving forward.

"That was generous of you," she said.

"What? We've got something. He's got nothing."

"You never give those guys money."

"A little here, a little there."

"You gave him five bucks."

"Five bucks?"

She nodded.

"I only meant to give him a dollar. Should I go back?"

"Honestly, Owen. Just try to pay more attention."

"Five fucking dollars."

"Let's go play some games."

"Sure, okay," I grumbled.

"How about the ring toss?"

"I'm not in the mood."

Supposedly frustrated by my supposed error, I suggested Whac-a-Mole. Conciliatory Patty, no fan of the game, conceded.

Five holes, a big scoreboard, a mirrored backdrop with a spinning yellow light on top, and a rubber mallet on a rope. I put my money in and hit play. The moles, brown plastic things with white buckteeth, popped out of their holes and I whacked them back in with the mallet, again and again. Patty played on the machine next to mine. Her score was consistently lower. She giggled as she hammered. I did not giggle. I stared at the five holes with cobra-like intensity. We played until Patty grew tired of it, and then I played two more games alone.

After that, we rode the carousel, which was a replica of the one Patty had ridden as a child, or so she remembered. We drove home and had a nightcap, then went to bed. We did not make love that night, both of us too exhausted, but the next morning began with a series of amorous embraces resulting in bad-breathed, bleary-eyed, sleepy sex that I would rank among the most satisfying couplings of our married years. Not since those early "love is a drug" days had my heart felt so completely given over to her.

We drank coffee together and looked over the paper, then she went shopping. I procrastinated for half the day, going to the car wash, et cetera, before returning to the quiet chamber of my home office via the Mailboxes Store. Lily and Raven, like twin Golden Retrievers, had been waiting for me faithfully the whole time. Moles, moles, get in your holes.

17

Lily

Moses said he sent you a letter but I didn't hear back from you yet. I was out-of-reach there for a while because of some incidents we don't need to get into. My biggest concern in life at this time is whether you got rid of Mr. Clancy yet because if you didn't I can see where this boat is going and I'd rather stay on shore.

As a matter of fact if you didn't get rid of Clancy good riddance stop reading right here.

If you're reading this now you got rid of that jerk and that's a good thing. I might seem rough around the edges but a lot of my actions are as a result of my having a bigger heart than most people. Some people say "Control yourself!" and I say to them "Don't you have any feelings at all?" because it seems like their whole lives they're trying to have NO feelings. That's who I am and your heart which I'm sure is plenty big does not have room for me and someone else. Trust me on that Lily.

As you probably figured out I was in the hole again. One of Stewart-Know-It-All's friends tried to settle the score in the middle of Group while I was talking. Group is stricter than other places so they put me away good for beating on him. He didn't get punished even though interrupting someone in Group is a punishable offense but with shrinks whoever cries loudest wins.

The whole time I was in the hole I thought about you and when I got out the guards said I seemed calmer in there than before. I used to scream and yell but they weren't shrinks. The squeaky wheel gets the grease but the nail that stands up gets hammered down.

I wrote most of this letter to you and then I was flipping through the poetry book and right there on page 86 Walt Whitman said it better than me:

As if a Phantom Caress'd Me

As if a phantom caress'd me,
I thought I was not alone, walking here by the shore;
But the one I thought was with me, as now I walk
by the shore—the one I loved, that caress'd me,

As I lean and look through the glimmering light—
that one has utterly disappear'd,
And those appear that are hateful to me, and
mock me.

That's exactly what it was like in the hole this time.
Do you know if Walt Whitman was ever in jail? It
seems like it. I don't think that other guy Richard
Lovelace was ever in prison even though he called one
of his poems "To Althea from Prison." Either he was
never in prison or he didn't have as big a heart as you
would think a poet should.

H

Dear Henry,

I got rid of Clancy, like you asked me to. He is, of course,
still teaching until Greta returns. I told him I thought
about his nice offer but I am otherwise attached. Yes, I
used the A-word: attached. I said before that I'd rather
have a real man where you are than a phony man out
here, and now I've put my money where my mouth is.

As for Clancy, don't worry; he took the news well
and has not tried to flirt with me since. As a matter of
fact, I think he has now set his sights on another
teacher. So much for steadiness of heart, huh?

I spent some time recently (I had the long weekend to myself) looking over the letters I've received from

you and I realized something. I've heard a lot of stuff about what's going on in there, and a little bit about your ex (boo!), and you've made some general points about the kind of guy you are . . . All well and good, by the way—a lot of you comes through between the lines. BUT at the risk of exchanging mystery for depth, I must ask you, especially now that I'm rejecting suitors out here, to share more of yourself. Who is Henry Joseph Raven? I don't even know where you're from, where you've lived, what your childhood was like, etc. Maybe they make you talk about this in Group and you're burned out? Or maybe you're a really private person? Or maybe (and this is probably most likely) we're just getting started? I don't know. But I want to know. What's your story?

A FAQ I read about writing to prisoners said not to ask about their crimes right away—that prisoners who felt like discussing them would do so of their own free will, but I think we've gotten to the point where I should know something more about what happened to land you in there.

I don't mean to sound cold (I hope I don't!) but if you want me, you're going to have to give a little more of you.

xo
Lily

PS Richard Lovelace was in prison when he wrote that poem, but I don't think he was in there very long. I don't think Whitman was in prison, ever, but he liked to use the Prisoner as a character in his poems.

PPS I wrote the above a day ago and I haven't mailed it yet, so this is an add-on. Something else happened to me when I went over our old letters. I realized I have not been entirely truthful with you. My father didn't really invent any plastics. He was an inventor, that much is true, but he was not as successful as I have made him out to be. I thought, when writing to you before, that I could convince myself that things were different, but I cannot. He was a good man. I suppose he was something of a dreamer. I have vague memories of his laboratory in the garage. I'm sorry to have burdened you with untruths, but you have to understand that I'm struggling with this myself. My aunt told me a different version of my father's story, that he was manufacturing drugs and selling them, but I refuse to believe her. You have to make your own version of events if you want to live a happy life. I just went a little too far.

xo

Lily

I found Patty packing up a file box in the living room. She had stopped wearing black altogether.

"What's going in there?" I asked.

"Old videos," she said.

"What's the point of packing away old videos? Everything is coming out on DVD anyway."

"CJ videos," she said.

"Oh." Did this mean I would no longer find my wife laughing and weeping on the sofa, watching increasingly static-filled images of her brother and his friends?

She looked up. "Don't tell my mother I'm putting these away, or she'll want them at her house, which will start a whole other cycle of her watching them, if you know what I mean."

I nodded. I'm not sure what I was thinking, but I found myself unable to speak, unable to summon the required platitudes.

"Are you okay?" she asked.

I nodded again.

"I can't keep doing this forever," she said. She asked for the packing tape, from the table.

I handed it to her.

"I just want things to get back to how they used to be," she said.

"Me too. That's what I want too."

She wrapped the box with packing tape and I carried it out to the storage shelving in the garage. I thought of my aunt's meticulous Eileen archives. Everyone's life is destined to become a bunch of boxes. We live, we leave behind a trace, the trace gets relegated to storage, we are forgotten.

It took me some time to realize what was going on with Patty. The way she had decided, as if on a whim, to suddenly stop mourning CJ, to pack his videos into boxes, was a clear indication that she was moving backward, emotionally. How can you console someone who refuses to admit she's hurting? She, whose inner life revolved around remembering her brother, had suddenly decided to forget him, to block everything out. Patty had always had that ability on a micro scale. She could pull herself out of any mood for the moment, if the situation demanded it. Now she was doing it with her whole life. She had given up, on some level unknown to her conscious mind, trying to find justice for CJ. That part of her which had nearly destroyed our sacred bond was being repressed even further. It would explode if not tended to. People die. Death is the mother of beauty, a poet said. We're all on the clock. Awareness of death is the mother of beauty. The death of others is the mother of beauty. My own death is the mother of nothing. My own death is the end of everything. An absurd idea. A joke that tells itself. Patty had excused herself from the burden of feeling. I was concerned for her.

18

Feverish at the Mailboxes Store. I was generally careful to keep my feelings in check, but somehow a flash of superiority at the Mailboxes Store snuck around my defenses and stormed my emotional citadel. There is something undeniably exciting about being in contact with a man who has taken another man's life. In my shoes you would have felt the same excitement. (My own sense of disgust threatens to censor me here, but if I cannot be honest, this is all a waste.)

The sight of my empty mailbox tempered my sense of superiority, with just enough disappointment to make me think twice about what I had been feeling. I was able to divide my feelings into three component parts and distribute them accordingly:

1. The allure of the killer. I assigned this part to Lily, as it would provide a useful motivating factor. She should be drawn toward whatever dark glamour attached itself to a killer.

2. The sense of superiority. This part—most keenly experienced among the people of the Mailboxes Store—I stitched onto my sense of mission. I was not going to stop until I had brought Raven to his knees, until I had made him feel what he had done, and to accomplish that I needed a somewhat inflated sense of importance.

3. The remainder, the excess, the part that threatened to overtake me, the sense that Raven had somehow become my killer—as if he were a starving child I was sponsoring by sending five dollars a month—I let myself feel as a reward for having done a good job so far, for having made, in a preview of the main event, Raven suffer a little bit already.

Someone said once that writing was like trying to dance with a bear who only wanted to wrestle. I'd gotten Raven to dance a few steps. He and I had become protagonist and antagonist in a world of minor players. What did the husband/wife-cum-brother/sister couple behind the counter at the Mailboxes Store have to do with it? What did my aunt and uncle have to do with it? Minor characters, walk-ons, bit parts, atmosphere. And Patty, what could she contribute now, really, while I was teaching the wrestling bear to dance, lulling him, seducing him, pulling him close, dancing cheek to cheek, until he himself wanted to dance, and then wrestling him to the ground . . . ?

This thinking of course resulted in an emotional hangover. Celebration of projected victories in the face of present setbacks is not recommended. In the midst of this aftermath, I realized I was leaving something out of the equation, something that would bring meaning to Raven's future suffering. It wasn't about me, my superiority, Raven's allure. It was about CJ. And he was disappearing. Patty was trying to put him away. I had met him only a few times. I remembered the polite disdain of a younger brother-in-law. An athletic build. A seemingly telepathic line of communication with his father, used primarily for inside jokes. Then he was gone and Patty, inconsolable Patty . . .

I left the Mailboxes Store and drove like a madman to the Stockings' house. I expected only the housekeeper to be there, but when I knocked, Minerva answered.

"Hello, Owen." She smiled in such a way as to ask what I was doing there. Not unfriendly, just inquisitive.

"Minerva—Minnie, hi. I'm sorry I didn't call. I just wanted—well, it's good you're here, anyway."

She invited me in, poured me a plastic cup of fresh-squeezed orange juice, the same kind I liked to purchase at the market we both frequented. I sipped from the cup and took a peek up the stairs. If she hadn't been home, I could have gone straight up to CJ's room. You can learn a lot about someone from the environment they create for themselves. I wasn't planning to ransack the place, but only to soak up the atmosphere, to refuel, to remind myself that CJ had once been a living human being.

"I'm sorry to bother you," I said, improvising, "but I wanted to talk to you about some things."

"I'm always here for you, Owen."

She made prayer hands at me and closed her eyes. It was a brief and spontaneous gesture, one I'd seen her make before, the intent of which was to convey blessings upon the recipient while also highlighting the humility of the one making the gesture. I hoped, for everyone's sake, that she wasn't going around town doing this, but one never knew. She did hang a dream catcher from the rearview mirror of her Escalade.

"I've been thinking about what you said to me at the market some time ago—about Calvin Junior and the leaf you saw falling . . ."

This was the only common ground I could think of that didn't involve other people. My first inclination had been to come to her with concerns about Patty's wardrobe change, but I quickly realized that (1) it didn't get me any closer to CJ's room, and (2) knowing Minerva, Patty would hear all about it before I even got out of the neighborhood.

"Oh yes," she said. "That was several months ago. He was right, too."

"Right?"

"The leaf can fall without bringing down the whole tree. That moment was a life saver. Literally."

How was I going to parlay this into a trip up to CJ's old room? Up the colonial steps, down the jute rug runner, second door on the left. I knew where it was, had been inside even, to dump and retrieve coats during a party for Calvin Senior's firm.

"How was it a life saver?"

"You're young yet, Owen. You don't want to know."

"Ironic that CJ is the one saving lives."

She nodded and dug up a smile. I was glad she'd remembered the leaf thing at all. The fact that she saw it as a life-saving event was even better, because while we sat upon the Early American furniture, I hatched a diabolical chick in my mental henhouse.

"I came here today," I continued, "without Patty—without even telling Patty I was coming—because I wanted to talk about CJ, just the two of us. I know I never knew him, really, but as the newest member of this family, I feel as though I have gotten to know the CJ you all knew. His light is far from extinguished—it is reflected in all of you. I feel honored, I guess is how I'd put it, to participate, even peripherally, in the stewardship of his memory. When Patty and I have children of our own—"

Her eyes lit up at this, as they always did.

"Not yet. Soon. I want to be able to tell those kids about Uncle CJ, whose life was taken way too early."

"I hope you'll be able to do that, Owen."

"I will."

"Fate allowing." She bowed her head prayerfully. "I don't mean to imply it isn't going to happen. On the contrary, I could wish for nothing more. But life doesn't always turn out like you expect, or hope. Fate's agenda is not always known to us."

"You can say that again," I said. I employ this phrase whenever I disagree with someone but want to imply enthusiastic agreement. All I have done is given the speaker permission to repeat their assertion. Despite the fact that I was about to unleash a string of careful untruths, I could not bear at that moment to hear myself talking about fate as if it were a real thing. Fate doesn't exist in real life. Sure, sometimes we see people setting themselves up for a fall unawares, but is that fate? Coincidence isn't fate. Character isn't fate. Fate, real fate, old-school Fate, is for characters in books and movies, not real people.

"I'm not quite sure how to say this," I continued, "but lately I've been feeling the presence—and let me know if this sounds ridiculous—the presence of someone, as if someone is watching over me, too."

"That's not ridiculous, Owen." She looked at me more clearly than she had ever looked at me before, with a yearning in her eyes. I became somewhat aroused by this yearning look of hers. I don't mean physically aroused, per se, but aroused in such a way that, if you pictured the mind as a 1950s supercomputer, the panel of lights reading "nonspecific sexual thoughts" lit up and began blinking, which it had never done in Minerva's presence before. The intensity of her gaze, the establishment of a newer, deeper connection between the two of us, our being alone in an empty house—all of these things conspired to set off my arousal mechanism for an instant, as when you see a woman struggling to push a shopping cart into the back of another shopping cart with her hips and you think to yourself "that is what she looks like when she is making love." No Oedipal web of connections, just a man and an older woman, and the "sex lights" blinking on and off for a millisecond. I wondered if Minerva's sex lights had lit up, too. I wondered if she'd ever thought of me in a sexual way, and this general wondering remained in my brain for some time. Minerva waited for me to continue—waited for me to validate her experience by repeating it back to her as my experience.

"Lately," I said, "I've been feeling a presence in my life, signals here and there, sort of like your falling leaf, and I have wondered more than once whether it might be CJ. Is that crazy?"

"It's not crazy at all." She got up and fetched herself some tissues. She did not return to the seat across from me but remained standing instead. She too, then, had felt the intensity of the moment, and felt safer a bit farther away. She wiped her eyes as she spoke, in that way women do, with the tip of her finger moving horizontally below the eye. (To keep mascara from running? Was she even wearing mascara?) "I've actually . . . you won't believe this, Owen, but I've actually been waiting for this since the wedding. We've all—even Cal Senior—we've all accepted you into this family. You've become a member of our family, and I knew it was only a matter of time before CJ would throw his blessing into the ring."

"It's generous of him," I said. "Especially considering I barely know him. I feel like there's so much more to know, like there's a whole room upstairs full of a life I've only begun to hear about."

"I'd be happy to help you get to know CJ better," she said. "I think it could be good for you and Patty, too, for you to know Patty better, by understanding who she lost."

I knew then that Minerva would lead me directly to the reliquary.

"What kind of signs have you been experiencing?" she asked. I had not the slightest idea how to answer this question convincingly, but I took my first cue from Minerva's own leaf-vision—a totally insignificant event, seemingly random and singular, imbued with significance for being random and singular.

"Please don't tell Patty," I said, stalling.

She nodded.

"I was sitting in the house a few weeks ago. And I heard a strange crashing sound, like dishes clanking in the dishwasher, followed by two thumps. Now, I couldn't tell exactly where it was coming from, in part because I wear earplugs while I work, but I first assumed that Asulcena had broken something again— she's unreliable, I think—and so I didn't leap up right away. Then

I realized she wasn't even there that day, so I thought: oh, no, one of the cats. But the cats were in my office, sunning themselves on my reading chair. I got up to investigate."

"What was it? Don't tell me—a car accident?"

"No, nothing like that. I walked into the front room and saw that one of our windows had been broken. Part of it was shattered completely, but the other part had the clean round outline of a baseball. I ran out front . . ."

"No one out there?"

"Deserted."

"Figures."

"I have literally never seen our street so quiet during the day. I look, I listen. No one. I get back in the house, annoyed at having to clean up the mess and call the glass guy and so on. While I was waiting for the glass guy—he came and fixed the window before Patty got home—I realized that maybe I should look for the ball. I had swept up all the glass, but for some reason I hadn't noticed the ball."

I should point out that Patty's stories of CJ's boyhood often referred to his love for baseball, and that he had more than once put a baseball through a neighbor's window. There was no reason for Minerva to know I'd heard those stories before.

"Because there was no ball?" she asked.

"Well, let's just say I didn't find it. I didn't look all that carefully, figuring it had rolled under something and would turn up later. I wasn't happy about the broken window interrupting my work, so I wasn't in the most receptive mood. But after the guy had come to fix the window and everything, I went back to my desk, and something that had been bothering me for weeks, a particularly thorny piece of documentation—no need to get technical here—all but solved itself, thanks to the broken window, I thought, and thanks to the ball. I decided I'd keep the ball as a memento of sorts. I went back out to find it, convinced I'd missed it before, and I tell you I turned the front half of the house upside down."

"There was no ball?"

"There was no ball." It took all my resolve to look Minerva in the eye and continue. "Just a sneaking suspicion, and I can't explain this either, that CJ had been involved, had paid me a visit somehow, to help me solve my problem."

"That sounds just like him," she said. "Breaking your window to help you out. He works in mischievous ways. Did so even when he was alive. Let me show you something." She indicated I should follow her upstairs.

I put down my empty cup, realizing only then that I'd been gripping it hard this whole time, and followed. Up the stairs, I first avoided, and then enjoyed, looking at her round and firm behind. My sex light panel did not light up. I noted the comeliness of her parts as a pleasant fact. The moment was not charged, as it had been earlier.

I knew where she was taking me. I knew what she was going to show me. Patty had mentioned it to me in passing once: CJ had a baseball collection, and it was still there, somewhere in his old room. He'd always been proud of his baseballs, signed and unsigned, old and new, and he'd held from an early age that such a collection was superior to a collection of statistical picture-cards that came with chewing gum, cards with no inherent value vis-à-vis the game of baseball. Patty cherished the collection quietly, as one of the things that made CJ CJ, and made his death that much more of a senseless tragedy. The world hadn't lost just another person, it had lost a CJ, and not only those who knew him, but the whole world (upon which he would have had some impact, had he lived) was the poorer for it.

Minerva led me directly to a window bench in CJ's room. She pulled the cushion off and deposited it gently on the floor. The top of the bench opened up like a chest, and she flipped it up with the flair of a magician's assistant. I could feel her eyes on the side of my head, scanning me for a reaction to what she'd revealed. To her, this scene was not about CJ's collection but about my reaction. It was about my being touched mystically by CJ.

I should have been bowled over by the clear sign of contact from the other side, all of these baseballs representing positive identification—CJ had visited me. And, had I been any kind of actor whatsoever, I might have performed that particular subspecies of wonder. I did not, because I could not contain my equally wonder-filled but far more mundane amazement at the baseball collection itself.

"That," I said, "is a lot of baseballs. Wow."

"He loved his baseballs, yes. But don't you see—"

Here my acting kicked in. To myself I felt very, very phony, but to Minerva—queen of apophenia, desperate for signs—I must have appeared convincing enough. I flashed my eyes wide in astonishment. "He loved his baseballs so much that they became his calling card. This is amazing. Confirmation that CJ was responsible."

"That's why I had to bring you up here, Owen. You realized only half of it. He was inviting you into the family."

I kneeled down to get a closer look at the balls and to shield my face from view, worried that I might betray the feeling of triumph I was experiencing in the face of what should have been a more solemn moment. The chest was full of baseballs, old, new, torn apart, boxed, even some signed ones in plexi cases.

"May I?" I asked.

Minerva nodded. I reached in and pulled out a ball: *Property of Mira Costa Little League.* Another: *Property of YMCA.* Another: *LEWIS* (in marker). Another: No markings, very old ball. A great number of the miscellaneous balls appeared to have belonged to someone else before coming into CJ's possession. I wondered if he'd stolen them.

"There's more," Minerva said. "Dig toward the bottom right. Be careful."

"A lot of balls in here," I said.

"Hold the door open," she said.

I held it open and she kneeled next to me.

"Remember how I was saying he was mischievous?" She rummaged in the corner of the bench. "Well, there was a period there where he was *really* mischievous." She retrieved a cardboard shoebox, an old Converse Chuck Taylor box, from the depths of the bench. Balls rolled down to fill the empty space. The box was labeled with a crudely drawn skull and crossbones and "CJs Stuff Keep Out." Minerva gestured at me to close the bench and I did.

She set the box on top and pulled it open.

Inside was a lighter, a can of non-dairy creamer, a roll of caps, a deck of playing cards with nude women on them, a dozen shaved-down pennies (all flat across Lincoln's head), and a lint-speckled piece of fake vomit. Also: a lone baseball with a small X written on it, under which he had written "CJ Stocking 1196 Maple Ave." Minerva retrieved a small spiral notepad from the bottom of the box.

"We weren't too happy when we discovered this. Somehow he'd managed to keep this a secret, even as he grew older. I think he probably forgot. Otherwise he would have mentioned it." She handed me the notepad. I opened it. The first page read:

Madlib #5
v: fuck
vpt: shitted
n: pussy
adv: fuckily
n: asshole
adj: gay
N: Cocknut Johnson
[...]

She shook her head. "Keep going—it's near the back."

I flipped through more Mad Libs, drawings of cars and explosions, clouds and lightning bolts, band logos (a VH with wings, etc.).

"There, take a look at that." It was a list of addresses:

X-ecutioner
1402 Apache (Susie)
310 Sassafras (Fred and Alex)
295 Oak (Kapil)

1356 Cherokee (?)
369 Myrtle (~~Millers~~)
371 Myrtle (Millers)

I stared at the page for a moment.

"It took us some time to understand it. Took us a while even to find it. I was in here reminiscing and came across it and didn't know what to think. Cal Senior figured it out finally. When he was a kid, CJ seemed to have the bad luck of putting baseballs through people's windows. And he was always afraid to tell us he had done it, so we would find out only when the home's owner, having read the address off the ball, came to our door during dinner, ball in hand, asking for money to fix the broken window. CJ would apologize and then—in front of the homeowner—work out some scheme to pay his father back as Cal Senior handed the man a few twenties, and then everyone would forget about it. Boys will be boys, right? Little did we know, CJ was keeping track. Still a bit of a mystery, really. We had a good laugh when we figured out what the list was. He was always up to something, that kid."

"Yes," I said. "Sounds like he was."

"So," she said. "There it is."

I looked at her, puzzled.

"There's the ball that came through your window. Should we enter your address into the book?"

I wrote our address into the book.

We put the ball away with the notebook in its box, cleared a space for it in the bottom of the bench, and laid it to rest in the corner, under a heap of baseballs eager to return to their original positions.

Minerva replaced the pillow on the seat and motioned for me to sit next to her. "I wouldn't have believed it either," she said. "But things like this have happened so many times."

I took in the room now, bookshelves first. There I saw senior year high school books—unread copies of *Lord Jim*, *Jude the Obscure*, tattered copies of *The Art of War* and *The Prince*. Yearbooks, high school and junior high. A small blank-spined black book—his journal?!—I longed to open and examine. A few photographs on the desk, family stuff, and a picture of him with a soccer ball, from some team he'd played on in his mid-teens. Posters on the walls: surf and music. Bed with matching dresser, desk, and mirror—a cream-colored lacquer bedroom set, circa mid-1980s. Baseball bat next to the bed (the only obvious sign of baseball in the room).

The coat hooks on the door were a big wooden C and J. They hung above a crudely installed deadbolt—hallmark of the territorial teenager. I was struck, of course, and this I had noticed upon first walking in, that the room didn't appear to have changed at all since CJ had lived there.

"I know what it looks like. I've heard it all. We need to move on, we should redo the room, put his things away for good. And, you know, I reply that we've got plans for the room, or that I can't bear to change a thing yet, and people turn supportive, Owen, they really do."

I nodded.

"Much more supportive," she went on, "than if I told them the truth. How would Nancy So-and-so down the street react if I told her the truth?"

"The truth?"

"We haven't changed the room because CJ won't let us—because he's still among us."

"Sure," I said. "Like the baseball. I was afraid to even mention it to you."

"About six months after he passed away, I came into this room and started to pack his things into boxes. I felt like it had been long enough, that his spirit had moved on. A dozen broken boxes, slamming doors, strange noises, and mysterious chills later, I decided to stop. This was more than a series of coincidences. It was CJ saying—like he always used to—'Mom! Leave my room alone!' He'd already been off to college for several years, you see, and we wanted to turn his room into a guest room—Patty's had already become a home office—but he wouldn't hear of it. Still won't. So that's why it looks like this. Not because we're having trouble letting go or something common like that. Because CJ wants it that way."

She was compelling, in the way that anyone can be compelling when they believe what they are saying. And as long as I continued to validate her experience, I could be assured of her cooperation and support. I had learned this lesson while working for software companies. At conventions, you could usually get people to talk about themselves after a few drinks at the hotel bar. A surprising number of very straight-laced, square people could be coerced into talking from that last cluttered corner of their minds, where a confused, underdeveloped, traumatized sense of spirituality had been packed away, and if you were supportive enough, you could get them to talk crazy for the rest of the night. They had no outlet, no voodoo ceremonies, no Latin Mass. I mention this now to clarify: I did not pity Minerva. I knew full well that most people carried around this kind of mystical mumbo-jumbo. Rather, I was flattered that she would share it with me. It could be argued that CJ brought us closer together.

She sighed. "I've got to get back to things downstairs." Her tone was such that she was not asking me to leave.

"Do you mind if I sit here a moment?" I asked. "This is powerful stuff, and I'd like to collect my thoughts."

She smiled a warm, motherly smile. "Stay as long as you like. You've been invited."

I watched her leave the room and close the door behind her. I had come here to remind myself that CJ had been a living, breathing human being, and that Raven's future punishments were the least I could do to avenge CJ's death. So (I asked myself) who was this young man whose life had been cut short so violently and senselessly?

Aside from the stories I'd heard, I knew very little. I'd learned a few things already: He might have been a baseball thief as a child. Also as a child, he'd enjoyed the destruction of others' personal property, and appeared to have engaged in it repeatedly, with few consequences. The mysterious "X" baseball was interesting to me not because it was or wasn't the ball from my made-up story, but because it was the first evidence of something darker in CJ's personality. He had repeatedly committed petty crimes, purposefully or at least negligently, had left his calling card behind, a baseball with his name and address on it, and had dismissed these crimes as accidents at least six times without incurring any worse punishment than his father's shaking head. Boys will be boys. Sounded like a brat to me, especially when one considers this additional detail from his college days: he wanted his room kept his way, whether he was using it or not. This was not the CJ I'd heard about, exactly, unless I'd misconstrued the meanings of "mischievous" and "rambunctious." Then again, who would call their dead son or brother *asshole?*

19

I stole CJ's journal. If he had been there, as Minerva believed he was, wouldn't he have made more of a fuss? I tucked it into my pants, made my escape, and took it directly to the Copy Store. (I later returned the original during a family dinner, after complaining that I had to use the toilet "in a serious way" and disappearing upstairs.) I was dying to examine its contents. At the Stocking house, I had only opened it long enough to ensure that it contained personal thoughts as opposed to a daily tally of events. At the Copy Store, I felt far too paranoid to pay the pages much attention. I looked forward to a leisurely read in the comfort of my home office. Unfortunately, I had Patty's "weekend" to contend with—she was off for two days. Worse, she had declared this weekend of all weekends as an opportunity to reconnect. Reconnecting seemed to me a difficult task. I was concerned for the moment with lives other than our own. In a mailbox one town away lay, potentially, a response from Raven, and in that potential response, some potential insight into the murderer and his crime. In my office, hidden in the shallow void of my desk's frame, below the lowest drawer, lay (again, potentially) the innermost secrets of Calvin Stocking Junior, murder victim, tragic loss. How could I be expected to focus on us? We were mere bench-warmers in this battle between life and death.

"I thought we should go to the Bathroom Store today," she said. "We can get a new soap pump and hand towels for the guest bathroom. Maybe a floormat. To sort of remodel it without remodeling. That would be fun, don't you think?"

"I'm on deadline."

"You told me we could go out together today. This is really important, Owen."

"Do we have to go to the Bathroom Store? Their parking lot is always such a pain."

"I'll drive. And it would be nice to have a project together."

"I guess."

"What's the matter?"

"I've just got to get in the mood. Right now I'm thinking that people are falling in love, people are cracking up, people are dying. It makes buying a soap pump seem sort of silly."

"Buying a soap pump with your wife is not silly. Especially when the two of you have not been spending enough time together. Especially when you've been overworked and overstressed."

"Fair enough."

That day, Patty dragged me to the Bathroom Store, the Lighting Store, and the Outdoor Furniture Store, the cumulative effect of which was so enervating, my entire identity turned to jelly, then liquid, which then leaked out of me until I became no one in particular. The rest of the weekend was only slightly more pleasant, but as far as she was concerned, we'd gotten a chance to reconnect.

I felt like a fraud.

If I could go back to that weekend I would set everything aside to talk to Patty about what was going on, about how she had started by changing her clothes and was now changing our bathroom. About how her desire to reconnect with me was akin to treating her symptoms instead of her disease. I would have talked to her about CJ, and her feelings about CJ, and what she was doing with them now, where she was storing them.

No, that isn't true.

If I could go back to that weekend I would attempt whole-heartedly to reconnect with Patty. I wish I could do so now. But I didn't, and I can't. I participated in body but not in soul, focused the whole time on what spoils lay ahead.

CJ kept this journal intermittently from his sophomore year of high school through the summer before he entered college, with a few scattered entries thereafter, all of them written while on break from college. I have reproduced the journal as accurately as possible ($\approx$95%) under the present circumstances. That said, the dating of entries below is entirely speculative.

CJ did not seem interested in capturing the rhythms of daily life. Most of the early entries appear to be borne of crisis, with some of the later ones recording matter-of-fact life changes. It is difficult to tell, especially in some of the later entries, what motivated him to pick up his journal and scribble a few lines. Overall, he wrote with admirable candor, either unconcerned that someone might discover his journal and read it, or unaware that his words, read by someone else, could have any effect whatsoever.

High School Sophomore Year

Why does fucken Patty think she's doing me a favor sticking me with her butt-ugly friend's butt-ugly sister? Patty's so high and mighty all the time, like an ugly senior should be better than a freshman hottie? DO NOT DO ME ANY MORE FAVORS LIKE CLARISSA "STINKY WINKIE" HYAMS!

Every time I write something in here I want to erase it but Mr. Blatz said not to. Or else it's useless. The something life is not worth living or whatever.

I stopped writing because I had nothing to say. But now I do: I am in love. A vision of womanhood. Her name is Anastasia Bertano. I don't know how to tell her or even if I should. I barely know Ana but I know she's having boyfriend troubles.

Mr. Blatz is always making us use words in sentences we make up. Here's one: I'm going to exacerbate Ana's boyfriend problems. Feeling demonic but fuck it. She shouldn't be with Jeff anyway. Found out from somebody (totally unreliable source) that the problem is he can't keep his boner hard. Plan A put into motion.

Plan A successful! They totally broke up.

Asked Ana out—she said yes! Oh I'm good.

Recap of 1st date with Ana (1 am right now): She talked about how bad it was at the end with Jeff and how her feelings were jumbled and crap like that. We made out for a while but she wouldn't let me touch her tits. She told me the boner problem thing was a lie and that she was a virgin anyway. Jeff couldn't handle Plan A, though, which was to have everybody limp when they walked past him at school, and so they broke up.

Ana = frigid. She won't let me touch her tits unless we're going steady but she doesn't want to go steady yet. I'm bored of her crap already so I told a few people (big mouths) that I fucked her and she was a dead fuck. I got Jeff to say it too after I told everyone the limp dick thing was bullshit made up by Marty Gelbart.

Could the waves suck any worse this summer?

High School Junior Year

Ana switched schools—how funny is it that like a year ago I was tying my stomach in knots about her and now I could give a shit? That's life.

Do your part for the War on Drugs: Kick a stoner's ass.

I don't know how it happened but I have a girlfriend already this year, Ana's ex-best-friend Denise. I saw her at Jeff's party. She said she was crushing on me all last year and then kissed me. I said if you like me so much show me your tits. We went into the pantry and shut the door and she pulled up her shirt. They were rad. She has already given me two hand jobs and said she would give me a blow job soon when we find a good place. I fingered her and she doesn't have a stinky winkie.

I HATE MY FUCKEN MOM! I HATE YOU MOM! I HATE YOU! Do not touch my shit any more! Leave me alone! I can't wait to go to college so you can <u>butt out</u> of my life!

Went to the Club with Dad tonight, got drunk. He went on and on with the "you're a man now" speech. In my head I was like: What do I get out of it? Anyway, he told me I could get a car now if I decided which ones I liked that were also affordable enough. I can't stop thinking about which one I want. He said no used cars so the Porsche is out. I think I want a Blazer or a Scirocco. The more I think about it, the cooler the Blazer is. Blazer. Yeah.

Got in a fight with Denise because she wants to follow me everywhere I go. Asked Dad about it—he said women are like that and you need to make boundaries for them. Talked to Jeff about starting up a poker night—guys only.

High School Senior Year

At the beginning of the summer I told Denise I wanted to play around some more but she just keeps coming back to me, which is fun for a while but gets annoying quick. I never learn. She thinks things will continue after high school but I can see from Patty and her new friends that <u>everything</u> changes. I told Denise today I like having sex with her and that's it. She started to cry and I told her to leave. I had to tell it like it was. She'll be back though and we'll go round and round. It's fun till I cum.

In deep shit. Rolled the Blazer. Dad said he'd take care of it but I had never seen him so bummed out. I am still pretty fucking drunk. Went to the club in the afternoon, hung out all day, drinking beers and whatever, finally got up the nerve to talk to this college chick who works behind the front desk. Played it cool like I was sober. She said we should go for a drive when she got off, which was half an hour later. We went for a drive and I crashed the car while we were messing around and driving. Luckily I didn't hit any other cars (we were in the canyons) and so there were no cops until after Dad got there. I asked Dad if the girl was going to get in trouble and he said not to worry because it wasn't my problem if she did. Look what she dragged me into, after all. I played "dumb kid" with the cops. Mom as usual overreacted and is trying to get Patty to talk to me on the phone from her job.

Unbelievable winter waves. Gulf of Alaska swells. College applications suck. I want to go to college in Hawaii but Dad says if I really want to surf the rest of my life, I'd better go to a good college so I can afford to someday.

Denise and I are really good, just casual. I'm not in love with her and she knows it so she doesn't ask. But it's all good again. She says I need to cool down and tune into the beauty of the universe. Booty of the universe.

I have to write my yearbook page stuff. I can't believe they want it so early. Patty had an idea for me to do the periodic table but with elements from my life. So far I've got: Good Waves, Panchos Tacos, Blazer, Family, Club, Jeff and Phil, Baseball, Mr. Meow, Denise (maybe?)

Haven't written in here in a while. Don't know why I picked it up tonight. So many things going on. "The best time of our lives." So many changes. This time next year I'll have already finished a semester of college.

Didn't end up doing periodic table thing. Couldn't fill all the spaces and the whole thing was way too "Patty" anyway. She gets all excited about an idea and then tries to make everyone else into another version of her. I think I'm going to major in political science. I told the career counselor I wanted to make a lot of money but I didn't want to major in economics cuz I hate my econ class so bad right now. Four years of that shit would suck ass.

Reggie Erb is on my shit list. If I kill him and go to jail, look here and see the reason why: At Monroe he hung out with all of us and played baseball. But when we came to Franklin High he got into theater and reading, which is fine. He has a shirt that he made himself: "Shakespeare Saved My Life." You want to speak a dead language and prance around in tights, okay by me. Live and let live, theater fags included. But today the prickmeister sees me walking down the hall and points at my varsity letter and says: "No way Calvin, you're a walking cliché," like he was some high and mighty judge of the school. I look at him and I don't know what to say because he's the cliché. So I say: "Sensitive, artistic, outsider, homo: cliché." He gets all excited and says I've proven his point, that I'm a typical varsity bully, etc. I walked away. We used to be friends before he thought he was better than everyone else.

Boulder! Far enough away from parents and Patty but close enough to drive home on breaks. All the snowboarding I can take. Plus it's a party school—Honorable Mention on the <u>Playboy</u> list. Killer.

Reggie Erb made fun of my <u>hard-earned</u> varsity letter, and I pointed out how unoriginal his <u>lazy pose</u> was. Who's the bully?

Patty brought home some guy named Luke to meet Mom and Dad. She says "it's serious" like he was on life support. I was hoping she would find a new type after college but no dice. Someone told me that chicks always want to date their fathers but that must be BS because in Patty's case the guys she dates are nothing like Dad. This loser was no exception. She picks the weak-spined ones, the ones she can order around. They can't get their shit together, so she gets it together for them. Like she wants a pet or something. She wants them to be there all the time so she can ignore them and not worry about them. I don't get it. She goes through them pretty quick b/c they end up having such boring relationships. She should get an iguana instead of a boyfriend, then she'd be happy. And a terrarium.

Luke the puke tried to chum up with me to gain an ally in the family. He's obviously afraid of Dad and inept at sweet-talking Mom, so I'm his only option. A typical weasel, looking to stick his nose in any open crack. I would give him a break if I liked him at all.

Patty is majorly pissed that Dad won't let her and Luke share a room. Luke "agreed" with Dad, which pissed off Patty even more. She stormed off and left me to hang out with her boyfriend. We played catch in the yard to get out of the house. I felt bad for him b/c he couldn't win either way in that argument. But I still threw the ball hard and he shook out his hand every time he caught it. I hope people at Boulder are cool.

College Freshman (Winter Break)

Pledged Beta (same as Dad)
Date parties rule!
Danced with ladies at old folks home on Halloween— smelled bad but was more fun than I thought it would be. Frat more than drinking and puking.

Wisdom in Beta house bathroom: "No matter how hot she is, bro, someone somewhere is sick of her shit!"

Trying to stay in touch with Jeff and Phil harder than I thought it would be. Made all kinds of new friends at school but also realizing how much of my life I owe to Jeff and Phil and how much I actually miss them. We played it cool in September, but now I feel like my life is getting super-slowly torn in two. Talked to Dad about it and he smiled and said "You're becoming an adult." We played golf after. Mom no longer on me about changing my room—I try to be more patient with her. Patty engaged to Luke but I don't want him as a bro-in-law.

College Freshman (Summer Break)

Saw Denise working at supermarket & pregnant!!! by some guy I don't know, older. Looks like she decided to go way blue collar (white trash) which surprised me. I knew she grew up in an apartment but still I thought she'd go to City College at least.

Good news! Luke broke off engagement with Patty. She's devastated but Dad and I agree she's better off. Dad told me he thought Luke was a fag probably, which I had not thought of.

College Sophomore (Winter Break)

Short break—going back early to ski more. All okay at home. Fun with Dad at club. Mom seems lonely, obsessed with cleaning my room. Patty dating everything that moves. Saw Reggie Erb in a dog food commercial. Laughed my ass off for a day and a half.

Things going great with Andrea. She's showing me the ins and outs of her home state. Lots of great places way off the beaten path. She has a built-in sense of adventure I really like. Have not used the L-word with her but probably will when I get back to school. Told her the other night on the phone that I was lucky to have found someone like her. She is very sweet but a ball-buster if pushed to her limit. I never thought I would find someone that sweet. She also makes things easy and doesn't complain about shit.

Patty seems to be over Luke. She didn't bring a guy home for Christmas but says she has three lined up as potential candidates. I don't even want to know, but she keeps pestering me for my opinion. Says she has to pick "the one" before she ends up alone forever.

College Sophomore (Summer Break)

Patty's looking for a new job, interviewing with biotech firms. She says she's a good candidate like she's running for president. I bet she'll get the job if she can focus. She finally found someone who wants to marry her, but he's older, a doctor, and he keeps giving her gifts without expecting anything in return, or so he says. She won't marry him.

Can't believe I'm only halfway through college. Then business school, probably. School never ends for me.

Only one week to go before Junior Year and Andrea called to tell me she has been seeing someone else in her hometown. Supposedly they just started up, but I bet it's been going on all summer. This really sucks. I can't stop remembering all the places we used to go. It's like a slide show in my brain, running alongside everything I'm seeing and doing.

I talked to Andrea and asked her what about us—didn't any of that matter to her? She says she loves me but that she also loves him. I will not be played like that. I am miserable. My heart is broken. Much drinking, golf with Dad. Mom sympathetic but useless.

The real unfairness is that she is the first girl I was ever ready to say LOVE to. I was gearing up to it. And now I've been dumped. The worst part about getting dumped like this is that I can see how she's played me, I can see what she was up to, and how weak and cowardly and lame it was, but I love her even more now than when we were going out. I want her so bad.

I couldn't be going back to school on a more miserable note. Mom is very angry on my behalf. Dad says that time will heal the hurt, and that everyone has to feel this way at least once. Some days I visualize returning to school and starting fresh—it's a big school, there are lots of chicks. I imagine what it would feel like if I had broken up with her. Other days I think I'll just revisit all the old spots we used to go and be depressed for a while. Let my system work it out. Or maybe I should just stay here and surf it off. Who wants to go back to school and explain everything to everyone anyway?

College Junior (Before Winter Break)

Well this has got to be the ALL TIME CLASSIC move! Home for a few days because PATTY GOT MARRIED without telling anyone and now Mom and Dad are throwing a party to make it seem legit. No one's even heard of the guy. She said they "just hit it off" on a ski trip and she knew right away that "he was the one." She found her iguana!!! Mom couldn't be happier. Dad thinks it isn't going to last. I think it shouldn't last but it will because Patty's so fucken stubborn.

Patty Patterson. I swear to god I laughed for a minute straight at that one.

At the party, Owen was crying and hugging everyone and going on and on about his "new family." I swear she must have found him in some animal shelter some-where. He hugged me and called me "brother." I didn't want to ruin his big day so I hugged him back.

Back to school tomorrow. Up late drinking with Dad. World Series postmortem etc. I brought up Owen. Dad said that it wouldn't break his heart if things didn't work out, but Patty had made her choice, and whether or not we think the guy is a dipshit doesn't matter.

Calvin Stocking Junior went back to school and was murdered nine days later, having been abducted, along with his car, from behind a roadside bar in the Rocky Mountains. I have been there. I sat at the counter at Diana's Grill and sipped a beer, pretending to watch the baseball game, thinking this was the last CJ saw of civilization; this was his jumping-off point. The bar was full of locals. A few hours later, the first Boulder sweatshirt arrived, and behind it, a steady trickle of Calvins and Andreas, looking for an authentic place to get drunk for the night. Raven's shadow fixed permanently on the wall. While writing Lily-letters, I returned again and again to the fertile ground of his journal because of one thing: Reggie Erb had been right. CJ had been a cliché, right down to the varsity letter. I don't mean to strip him of his right to be a complex human being—there were glimpses of that even in some of the later entries, but it has always amazed me how well-defined he was as a person, even to himself. On the big issues he was uncomplicated. He knew who he was, knew what he wanted, and knew how he felt. There was no doubt in him.

I was all doubt, and coming face-to-face with CJ in the mirror-texts of his journal threw me into a whirlwind at the most fundamental level. I had no idea what came next. I couldn't help but admire CJ's sense of certainty. It made me wonder how he faced death when in those final moments he knew it was coming for him.

20

About a week after I first read CJ's journal—I read it many times, as an object of study, as a motivator—I walked into our living room from the kitchen and found that Patty was no longer in front of the television, where I'd left her, but absorbed with something in the front window. She had pulled the curtains back (we always kept them closed once the sun was down) and appeared to be concentrating intently on something outside.

"Everything okay out there?" I asked.

"Sure," she said. "I'm looking at the window, though, not out of it."

"You're looking at the window?"

She turned to face me. "Which one of these panes did the baseball go through?"

"The baseball?"

"Yeah, my mom told me some story about a baseball breaking one of our windows. Which one was it?"

"One of the middle ones," I said.

"Which one?" Patty's tone didn't seem suspicious, just curious. Still, I was wondering where this was going.

I pointed out one of the panes. "That one, I think."

"The window guy did a good job," she said, examining the mullions.

"He seemed like a pro. Quick, too."

She was looking into the pane now, watching me through the reflection.

"Did you tell my mother you thought CJ had broken the window?"

"I told her I couldn't find the ball."

"You didn't tell her you thought it was CJ?"

"She has a way of suggesting things. I didn't want to contradict her."

Patty rolled her eyes, returned to the couch, de-muted the television. I sat down next to her, asked her if everything was okay.

"I don't need you encouraging her," she said.

I apologized, and we watched television, but the tension remained in the background. Not wanting a lecture on CJ, I didn't mention it the next day, and neither did she.

Soon afterward, we were at a friend's brunch, sitting around a large picnic table, when a girlfriend of our host burst into tears. Her mother was dying. As soon as the subject came up, Patty was poised for action. The rest of us said "sorry" and "our thoughts are with you" while Patty said "losing someone really sucks" and then told the story of her little brother's murder.

Only then did I realize that she had begun using the same words to tell the story every time, that I knew every twist and turn, knew the way she held the trump and waited until the last second to play it.

Murder trumps cancer.

Brother trumps parents.

Patty had no idea how automated she'd become. Only someone like me, close but outside, could see the patterns. A marriage fails or succeeds based on what one does with those patterns. An average wife has to listen to fishing stories, an average husband has to hear about the latest shoes, and we learn to respectfully tune out our spouses' pet fancies. But this was no fishing, no shoes. This was a major traumatic event, as big as big deals get. And she'd turned it into rote. Her shields were going up. No amount of analysis or discussion is going to change us. Life is a plane crash—you know you're going down but you can do nothing to stop it. Patty was curdling. I was trying to bring my wife back from the world of unfeeling.

I drove to the Mailboxes Store, in search of my antagonist, all the while thinking that this project, this bringing-Raven-to-his-knees, would be the icebreaker to crack Patty's frozen seas before they icified forever. I was trying to save our marriage. I was trying to rescue CJ from the pat stories that threatened to eclipse him as he was. I was trying to wake everyone up. I was running around a burning house in the middle of the night, screaming "get out" before the whole thing came crashing down. I was poised for battle, my steed Lily Hazelton snorting steam in the early morning air, cantering toward the inner chambers of the murderer's heart, cold blood meets colder, to blow it up from the inside. Again at the mailbox, again turning the key, becoming the key, opening the lone envelope. I am the man who penetrates hearts. Patty's, to nourish it. Raven's, to destroy it.

Dear Lily

When you have a bigger heart than other people you have to be a private person. Otherwise you're just going to end up in trouble. Don't worry about getting to know me. I am private but I am not all closed up inside like some people I know. I have been careful with you. I will not fall for the same trick twice. I mean my ex. I am happy you got rid of Clancy.

You will never know me and I will never know you. But we all try don't we. You asked me what happened to land me here and frankly I probably wouldn't have told you unless you asked because it is a sad stupid story.

I am not much of a storyteller unlike some friends of mine. I have never liked to boast or make things out to seem more to my benefit. I've seen too many liars in my life and I have always considered bending the truth to be an ugly quality like having a rotten tooth.

I didn't kill anybody.

Now that I have spoiled the ending of my story I will tell you the rest. You know what they convicted me of but I wasn't the one who did it. If I was going to kill someone NOW it would be Hoden B Murray aka the asshole who put me in here by falsely snitching.

We were drinking and rolling from bar to bar and generally being up to no good. I see now how I took my life for granted even if trouble does follow me around it's a lot better than being caged up. We were up to no good anyway but we didn't mean anyone any harm. My pickup wasn't working right so when we tried to leave Diana's Grill we couldn't get it started. That's the pickup you saw in the picture—a good and reliable truck except that night. Murray says hey let's go back to the bar and see if we can borrow someone's car. I say sure.

Well nobody wants to lend us their car. Time for Plan B I said. Now you'll see that I mean to tell the truth always because I'm not afraid to face the shameful things I've done. I look at those things face to face and I consider them real hard. Prison isn't made for rehabilitation at all but that's what I'm trying for. We went around back of the bar and waited just outside the light there. Guys were always coming back there to drain the weasel because there was only one can inside and the college kids who came to Diana's generally could not hold their beer. So we waited there in the shadows watching the bugs fly into the light and bounce off. I said fuck it Murray let's go back in and drink some more. But Murray had hatched a Plan B of his own after hearing me say Plan B. I never had a Plan B really.

The music got loud for a second then I looked up to see this college kid coming out the back door. He stumbled down and stopped to let the wind hit his face. He staggered over out of the light to where everyone used to take a leak and I'm standing there waiting for the right moment. Murray runs up and tackles the guy as soon as he's standing in the dark. This should give you some idea as to how fucking stupid Murray was. He brings the kid down in a puddle of piss and the kid is pissing all over himself and Murray asks the kid if he has a car. The kid says fuck you so I walk over and point the gun at the kid. The three of us walk to the kid's car and Murray drives while I hold a gun to the kid in the back. He stinks like piss so we drive with the windows down. He wants to know where we're taking him but I don't know and Murray's not telling. Again I know that this was criminal behavior and stupid on top of that. We would have left the kid in the parking lot of Diana's Grill except we would have gotten caught too quick. We were just looking to have a little fun. We drove upstate a ways. The kid threw up a few times and cried for a bit. But he could see we were just having fun and I think he figured that if he helped us have fun we wouldn't shoot him. He started telling jokes. He told all kinds of jokes. Helen Keller Polack Nigger Fag Beaner Leprechaun. You name it. He wasn't funny at all. He couldn't tell a joke but we laughed anyway because we couldn't believe this piss-soaked kid thought telling jokes was going to get him out of this. Murray kept driving until the kid ran out of jokes. He must have told us every joke he ever heard all the way down to the Vampire ones. My favorite one of all came near the end. It gets funnier the more you think about it which is the opposite of most jokes: Why did the cow roll down the hill?

Because it didn't have any legs.

Who the hell knew where we were when the kid ran out of jokes and Murray pulled over. I tell the kid to walk out into the forest. It's pitch black except the light from the car. We walk through some trees and there's an open meadow. The kid was crying again. He thought I was going to cap him but all we wanted was use of his car a little longer and this was the best way to keep him occupied. So I say to the kid Run but he doesn't run anywhere. Don't shoot me he says. Run I say and I point into the darkness. He starts off kind of slow which was too slow for my taste so I shot the gun into the air. Nowhere near the kid. He hauled ass into the woods. I could hear him stumbling. I laughed real hard until I heard the tires screeching away.

Murray thought I shot the kid which I did not.

What happened next was that I walked for a long ways by the road until a trucker gave me a ride into the nearest town. I don't know if you know towns out here but it was not the friendliest place. When I woke up in their park in the a.m. the Sheriff was already riding my ass. My head was pounding cause of too much drink. I was sure the Sheriff was going to take me in for stealing the car or dropping that college kid in the woods but to my surprise and relief he hadn't heard anything and just drove me to the bus depot and told me they didn't need my type around their town. Little did I know I would see him in court later and the whole morning would become public record.

From there I bussed it home where I eventually got my pickup and fixed the problem aka the alternator. When I found out I was wanted and Murray had snitched and the kid was dead I did what any sane person would do and took off hoping they would clear it all up before they found me. Which as you know is not what happened. The deed got pinned on me because of circumstantial evidence. I know what I did was wrong and I'm fine doing the time for what I did but I don't need to be doing someone else's time on top of that. I also know the evidence against me was strong enough to convince a jury and if I had been in that jury I would have been convinced too. Stupid Murray got scared and made things sound worse than they were. He probably still thinks I shot the kid out there but who in his right mind would kill that kid for no reason in the middle of the woods? Not me. I liked his jokes even though he wasn't funny. I think he got hit by a stray hunter's bullet. I threw my gun in a lake when I was on the run but they didn't try to fish it out to prove that the bullet wouldn't match my gun. Instead they planted bullets at my house to match the bullet they found in the dead kid. They call this BALLISTICS. I call it framing an innocent man with hocus-pocus. The system doesn't want to prove my innocence. I bet it's too late anyway and the gun has rusted away otherwise I'd ask for your help in getting it out of the lake and clearing my name once and for all.

I told you it was a sad and stupid story. Sad cause a college kid got killed. Stupid because a little goofing off with no harm meant to anyone ended up with me being incarcerated. That's my story and since my hand is cramping I'm going to sign off for now.

Love
Henry

PS Next time I'll write more about my past like you asked. But first you have to tell me more about yourself specifically something to help this lonely inmate get through the night if you know what I mean.

Of course, Raven killed CJ. He lied blatantly to Lily while pledging himself to openness and truth-telling. How I wanted to confront him directly! But now was the time for Lily to get suckered by Raven, to let him seduce her, until he thought he had her in his clutches, and then to tear her away from him.

Seduction works both ways. Even when the so-called seducer is at his most calculating he is being drawn inexorably into a trap built for two. The more she gave herself over to him, the deeper he would step into the trap, which, as I had planned, would snap down as Lily—as deep into it as her counterpart—disappeared into a poof of particles, a magician's cloud of smoke.

In this scenario, I stand to the side, the magician, manipulating the mirrors that make the illusion possible.

There was a minor victory at the end of his letter, no question about that. He had signed it "love." Whether he meant it as a gesture of goodwill, an impulsive expression of feeling, or a calculated move to harvest from his correspondent some masturbation fodder, he had, by writing that four-letter word, exposed himself. Even if he considered it a cool and opportunistic stratagem, there lay behind that word the desire for a response, the expectation of a response, the notion that he was not writing into the void or even to an irregular correspondent but to someone he could expect something from. He'd gotten hooked, a bit, whether he knew it or not.

For that, Lily would throw him a bone.

I went to work modifying a new photograph, a woman, tan and youngish but not firm, standing poolside at what appeared to be a desert hotel, wearing a yellow bikini. I'd found her by searching an image bank for the word "poolside" and scrolling through 376 personal photographs. My initial search, "bikini," had yielded a surfeit of soft porn and assorted images of pin-ups, hot-rods, underwear advertisements, anime, a very fat woman, and a mushroom cloud over the Pacific. The woman's face, to be covered by Eileen's from a hiking snapshot, made me think of the schoolteacher's brand of strict cheerfulness. I visualized that impression shining through a sort of digital palimpsest, to suffuse Eileen's image with a dash of Lilyness.

The creation of this latest Lily led me again through all the photos I'd scanned of Eileen. With each new image came a flood of memories, some of them of moments I knew I had not witnessed. Part of me could see them as if they were a movie playing in my head, while another part cried out across the chasm to remind me that I had not been present at these events. Other memories were real, and those rose like zombies from a graveyard, staggering across my consciousness, each demanding a piece of my brain.

Eileen used to call me late at night and tell me about the situations she'd find herself in. Ditching a stolen car in the LA river, stripping in the VIP room at a club, leaving an OD at the entrance to the ER, and so on. I wouldn't hear from her for months, and then she'd call three nights in a row. She needed to talk it out, she'd say. She needed an audience. I was always there for her. When she died I half-expected the phone to ring at 3:00 a.m.: "Dude, you'll never believe where my soul ended up . . ."

The word *ghost* should be like the word *pants*—it should never be singular. No one leaves behind one ghost. Everyone who dies leaves behind at least as many ghosts as people they knew. I had been sidetracked in my Lily-making by two dozen of Eileen's ghosts, and when they were finished with me, I turned my thoughts to the ghosts that had been haunting me more recently, those radiating from Calvin Stocking Junior. I had wanted to know how this young bastion of certainty, this brat, this loved one, this window-breaker, had fared in the last moments of his life; if Raven was to be trusted on the details not pertaining to his guilt, I now knew. He vomited, cried, told every joke he knew, cried again, and turned toward the darkness when ordered to. Then, according to testimony provided by two independent forensics experts, Raven shot him in the back of the head.

21

Dear Henry,

I appreciate your honesty. Thank you. And I'm sorry if I seemed to be preoccupied about not knowing you. It's not easy waiting for your letters. I had a few drinks tonight in preparation for this one. I must say I debated whether or not to share my fantasy with you just yet, but then I thought about what I asked you and how open and honest you were in writing about it, and I decided I should respond honestly to whatever you ask of me. It's just you and me, after all. I hope you won't be offended that it took three cranberry and vodkas to get me to write this, but it's personal.

I have many fantasies, and I like to change them often, but there are a few I return to again and again. I used to picture a man without a face, but now I let myself peek with my mind's eye and there is a face—yours. I am not

ANTOINE WILSON

one for wide-open places in my fantasies. In regular life
I love nothing more than looking at the ocean spread all
the way across the horizon . . . but let me get on with it.
I'm afraid, I think, to write it down . . .

I am getting ready for school. It is early morning,
and though I've showered and done my hair, I'm still
wearing my robe. I hear the doorbell. I tighten my robe
and look through the peephole. It is you, but you are
wearing an electrician's uniform. The shirt is tight and
barely restrains your muscular forearms. I watch you
through the peephole as you ring the bell again. I take
a deep breath and reach for the knob. I know that as
soon as you are inside you will be in control. I open the
door, half-expecting you to ravage me right there, but
you ask me where the problem is. I say the outlet in
the bedroom is not working. We go to my bedroom
and you test the outlet. It's dead. But you soon figure
out that it is connected to a switch on the wall. You
begin to explain it to me then realize—this is my favorite, watching it dawn on you—that I know all about
the switch. I called for another reason.

You put down your tools and approach me. We
stand face to face for a long while. I reach out and touch
the front of your shorts. There is a substantial bulge
and it feels hot to my hand. I unzip your fly and pull
out your thing through the front of your pants. I play
with it until it feels like it is about to burst through your
skin. Your fly pushes on your balls and your thing is
super-hard. You look at me now. You are thinking of

what you want to do to me. You reach for the belt of my robe and I think you are going to loosen it, but you pull it tighter. You take my shoulders and turn me around to face the wall. You do this gently but with total authority.

You press me against the wall, not violently, but with a good amount of pressure, so that my cheek is against the plaster. You pull my belt tight again. You reach under the back of my robe to touch me. I have never been so wet. You pull the robe up and enter me from behind. You push and push me against the wall, and we move sideways until we are in the corner of the room. You're pushing me into the corner now. I am full of you and I am being pushed by you and by two walls. You groan and I like it. My knees collapse and you come down to the floor with me. You fill me and push me into the corner at the bottom of the two walls. My head is where the walls meet the floor and you are pushing from above and behind and the walls and the floor are pushing back and this is where I usually have an orgasm.

I can't believe I told you all that but I'm going to drop it in the mail right now before I reread it or tear it up. I have never written that stuff down for anyone, Henry, including myself, so you're the first one to have me like this. Please write back to me very soon as I will be worried all week about how this letter will be received.

Love back,

Lily

PS In your last letter you mentioned that you had to spend the night in a park, and that the police woke you up and ran you out of town. This is the most unlikely of coincidences, Henry, but I too have spent the night in a park only to be awakened by the police. I was a teenager, and I had run away from my aunt and uncle's house for the night. I stole a sleeping bag from a sporting goods store and rode the bus until the end of the line. I slept outside, in the cold, and I was happy because the outside was matching up with the way I felt inside. I can't help but think our shared experience is a sign.

Lily's letter, apparently written in haste and sent off immediately, was actually composed over several nights, as I tried to fine-tune the raw but still Lily-like language and, more importantly, the subtext of Raven's growing power and domination over Lily. Yes, Raven, dominate her! She is yours, make her precious and constant in your mind, take her for granted, visualize her, sexualize her, fetishize her, entwine your heart with your image of hers! Nibble at the cheese while you can—the spring will come to break your neck.

I knew Raven well enough to know that further masturbation over pictures of Lily, or better yet, over the mental vision of Lily, could only cause her to loom larger in his mind and heart, could only sink the hooks deeper into him, and make the tearing away that much more painful. And I knew that the more vulnerable I made her, the more powerful I made him, the better chance he would really enjoy it.

In constructing Lily's fantasy, I made sure to blend elements of women's fantasies gleaned from old girlfriends (the faceless man, the emphasis on context and story) with the more male-centered imagery of domination and bondage, not to mention a physiological focus and general pressure-building. Still I felt as though I had only scratched the surface.

Rereading it, I thought it a little cursory somehow, probably because it had taken me so long to compose—I expected it to take as long to read as it had taken to write. The composition period was strenuous, given the type of research I pursued—an issue of an octavo-size narrative-form porn magazine—and the necessity of relieving my own pressures along the way. I couldn't help but picture aspects of the situation Lily had written about, and I couldn't help but become aroused by them.

Once, on a time-out in the bathroom, I pictured myself in the electrician's uniform, pounding away at Lily, then Eileen, then Patty, as she moved from a one-dimensional wall, to a two-dimensional corner, to the three-dimensional meeting place of two walls and the floor. I had not planned to step into Raven's shoes like that.

22

I went into the office to submit some of the documents I'd been working on. Despite all the Lily-Raven correspondence, I was actually ahead of schedule. I have always been a natural at writing, so I was able to rush chapters without compromising quality. Neil missed having me around the office. He needed the security of seeing me actually work on the project alongside him. A normal human impulse, but one that led him to impugn the quality and timeliness of my work.

"You've missed deadline on the last two chapters, Owen. I know it's been a rough time, but I need you to speed it up. When you're late, the graphics-and-layout deadline doesn't change. I'm the one who gets crunched."

"I'll tell Peter to give you more time."

"No matter what, I'm going to have to pull all-nighters to get these chapters done."

"I'll get on it. I'm sure Peter will be sympathetic."

"He wasn't happy with the last chapter. I told you the text was a mess."

"It's all there, Neil. Don't sweat it."

"You can't just stick in your aphorisms and think they're going to slip by the editors."

"Live a little."

"I need the last two chapters."

"What's your favorite joke?"

"Do you have the last two chapters?"

"Have you got a favorite joke?"

"You're not going to start slipping jokes into the manual?"

"Why did the cow roll down the hill?"

"You're going to get us both fired if you keep this up."

"And someday you're going to die."

"Jesus, Owen."

"What's going to happen then? Isn't that worth thinking about?"

"I'll leave that up to God, thank you."

"When you die, the world dies with you. Nothing to learn, no reward or punishment, not even the sensation of drifting through blackness. Think about that for a minute."

"Yeah, well, that's not what happens as far as I'm concerned, plus I'm short on time right now. Have you got the chapters or not?"

"I emailed them to you when I heard you get up from your desk."

"You think that's funny?"

"Have you ever been heartbroken?"

"Thanks, Owen, I'll be in my cubicle."

I stared at my computer for a while. There was more work to be done.

It could wait.

Dear Henry,

I know I just sent you a letter, but I couldn't resist writing again. I hope that when you are gripped by the impulse you will do the same. I wanted to share something with you. In our classroom we have a large terrarium, with an iguana inside. The kids named him Eduardo. He is a sweet iguana and he's wonderful to have around. The other day, after all of the kids had gone home, when the school was quiet, I was grading some quizzes and I heard him scratching around his terrarium. I walked over to watch him eat and drink and I noticed something when the angle of the light changed. The glass of the terrarium was marked up with the children's handprints and nose-prints. All I could sense was that those children would all be gone someday, returned to the earth, and I began to cry. Not for their eventual departures, but for those smudges left on the glass. I don't think those smudges would have been as beautiful if those children were going to live forever. My sense of what is beautiful and what is sad and what is to be protected is nowhere reflected in the world around me. Only in those moments when I find myself alone with, say, an iguana and a terrarium, do I feel like I have any sense of my true feelings.

I had to tell someone about it, someone who would understand, and I don't have anyone but you. Write back soon!!!

Your Lily

23

Patty was concerned about me. I could see that. She suggested I take a day off and join her father at a baseball game. He was leaving work early, she said, and the seats were supposed to be excellent. I was not overjoyed at the prospect of an entire afternoon alone with the imposing if affable Calvin Stocking Senior, and the prospect of doing so at a sporting event was like a multiplier to my anxiety. On the other hand, there is a certain pleasure to be gained when accompanying someone as a guest to an event they hold sacred, and while venturing downtown, finding a good parking spot, and navigating the stadium sounded to me like a series of horrible headaches, they were for Calvin Senior suffused with anticipation. It didn't hurt that he had season tickets, a powerful air-conditioned sedan, and preferential parking.

In the few instances when I have witnessed a professional baseball game in person, the most exciting moment for me has always been when I step from the walkways of the stadium's vendors into the seating area, and, slowly, as if a curtain is rising, the overhanging seats above recede as I walk to my row, and the field, with its white chalk, red soil, and green grass, reveals itself. It's like entering a new room in a museum not knowing that the painting you are about to see is one you've admired many times in reproductions, and it reveals itself to be so much more vivid than you ever thought it could be. So it was, after Calvin Senior and I had purchased our hot dogs and beer, when we entered the seating area itself.

"Wow," I said.

"Yep. They're up by three. Must have been some first inning."

If Calvin Senior had any aesthetic reaction to the stadium, it was well-concealed under the pleasure he took in the game itself. For me the game was a slowly winding-down re-veiling of the beauty initially unveiled by our entering the stadium. But this was because I was constitutionally uninterested in the scores, the tactics, the plays of the game. I knew CJ would have joined him in a higher appreciation of the game and I tried to pay attention to the players, understand who was good and why. Lest I sit there constipated-looking, I injected a comment or two and waited for Calvin Senior to agree or to correct me, the latter occurring more frequently. On the finer points, he patiently explained why I was wrong, but on the fundamentals he couldn't help but give me a look of complete disbelief, a where-have-you-been-all-this-time look before shifting back into teacher mode. With each comment I dared assay, I knew I was putting myself in greater danger, but I couldn't help myself— I wanted to help ease his pain a little, help him understand that he still had a son of sorts, albeit a poor replacement for the one he'd lost.

During the happy seven innings our team was leading, I would hear the crowd cheer, and I would cheer, and he would look at me with a look of unadulterated joy and release, cheering too. He was sharing a sports moment with me. We were bonded as fans. He had found in me that thing he had only shared with CJ. Then the crowd would quiet down and I would stupidly open my mouth and say something to demonstrate that I did not understand the ramifications of a play, and our house of cards would fall. Our talk would resume as it always had, questions like "How's the manual coming?" and "How's life with my daughter?" to which I answered "great" and "great," no further elaboration required, or chitchat about what he called "the good life," on which he dispensed advice of the "always drink the fancy stuff" variety. Then the crowd would cheer again, and we would get caught up in the moment again, and I would try to say nothing stupid. I would never be the Junior to the Senior. We both knew it, but we couldn't help trying, our failed attempts at connection the only testament available, the only way to demonstrate our good intentions toward each other. It's as close as I ever came to having a father.

The other team found a burst of energy near the end and came back; within half an inning their victory was assured. Calvin Senior sulked on the way to the parking lot. Had the loss of the game dragged his mind into other dark places? I tried some conversation.

"Big parking lot."

He didn't respond. We weaved through rows of cars. He stopped short.

"You see this car?" he asked.

"Sure," I said.

"Chevy Blazer. CJ's was silver. Look at this piece of shit." He put his hand on the hood, turned his face toward me. "You know why they killed CJ, don't you?"

"I don't know the details, no."

"They killed him for his car. Look at all these fucking cars, Owen. Cars are everywhere. This city is stuffed with cars. They killed him so he wouldn't tell anyone who stole his car. So they could drive around a while longer."

Killing someone for a car seemed like the most absurd thing in the world right then, like sitting in a mountain lake and killing someone for a sip of water. He turned and continued walking until we reached his sedan. He had positioned it so we could exit the stadium easily without having to sit in too much traffic. We didn't talk the rest of the way back to his office, where I'd left my car, and I felt as though I had failed in every way as a substitute CJ, as a random person to enjoy a game with, even as a confidant son-in-law, but when Calvin Senior dropped me off—he wasn't going back to his office—he gave me a big smile and a firm handshake and thanked me for coming with him.

"That was really fun. We'll do it again," he said, and I thought that while in substance I had failed, in sentiment I had succeeded. I was slowly becoming, vis-à-vis Calvin Senior, one of the guys, his boy, even.

"I had fun, too," I said. "And I look forward to learning more next time," an innocuous phrase by which I somehow, yet again, highlighted the distance between us.

He tried his best to look unfazed. "You bet," he said.

I headed toward home, but when the turnoff appeared, I didn't take it. I had to check the PO box. I'd meant to leave it for the next day, but I couldn't stand the idea of Raven's response lying there unread all night.

Dear Lily,

Thank you for the picture and the letter. You have made this man less lonely all right! You know what I actually thought the other day? I thought I wouldn't know what to do with myself if you weren't there for me to write to. I know I need to keep up my end of the bargain too and tell you some more about my childhood and all that but be patient with me. As you guessed we do talk about it in group and I don't always want to rehash everything all over again partly because I'm tired of it and partly because it doesn't do me any good. I know I owe it to you and I end up giving it to them where it does me no good. It would be better to give it to you. The story of my life could find a home in your warm heart. What happens in group is a whole lot of talking and they never quite give you the reason why.

I am living proof that talking about it doesn't make a difference. I have an idea that we're like a house and our mouths are like the sprinklers. The heart is a washing machine in that house, tumbling the same stuff around week after week. You can talk until the front yard is flooded and the washing machine still works the same. I know some people like that. All the talking in the world doesn't make a difference. Unless you are really into fooling yourself which I'm not.

I'll tell you something your letter did to me and that was throw me into a fantasy of my own. You got me thinking about the outside again which I'm always thinking about I guess but I don't really listen to myself usually. So you wrote a double fantasy because after I was done with your letter I pictured myself driving around in my red pickup in an electrician's uniform with all the tools I would need. I pictured myself leading a normal life with trees in it. Maybe some kids someday. I pictured myself back at home with my tools in the green shed with white trim and fishing in the crick through the ravine behind the house. For once I could slow down and do something like work on the vegetable garden. I picture rows of carrots and turnips and tomatoes down the side of the ravine. So different than this place where even from the yard you can't see anything. They put us flat in the middle of nowhere. You can't even see the mountains.

Whatever happens between us Lily take one piece of advice from me: Boredom is a small price to pay for a normal life. I could never handle that boredom when I was younger. Now I would welcome it in a second. My life right now is fear and aggression and routine. I welcome every letter you send me because you and only you help me dream of a better life. When I am reading or writing our letters I am not in prison but somewhere else. So you can see why I'd rather talk about the future than my past. In here you're always thinking of the outside and always trying to keep yourself from thinking about it—otherwise you would go insane which I've seen happen more than once.

But when you write about the outside I feel like I'm already out and walking with you on that beach. I don't know why I'm going on and on like this but maybe it's because of the courage of your letter— maybe I want to match your courage and open my closed-off places to you like you did for me. You said in your letter that I was the first to ever have you like that. When I talk about courage that's what I mean. I want to be able to write to you and be able to say truthfully no BS that YOU ARE THE FIRST TO HAVE ME THIS WAY except I wouldn't be writing about my fantasies but the reality of my past. I look forward to doing that Lily I do. Please don't think any less of me if I can't find the courage right now. Write back soon.

Yours
Henry

Should I admit that my hands were shaking as I read Raven's letter in the Mailboxes Store parking lot? The lack of structure, the soul-searching—Raven had let his guard down, and what's more, he admitted as much at the end of his letter. He was looking for the courage to open up to Lily. This was a big step forward from his CJ story, which had seemed like a breakthrough at the time. But while before I had been impressed with his garrulous openness, I was now far more impressed with his equally garrulous closedness—because he was struggling. This was no story-dump. This was a man actively testing his own limits—all for Lily. I did not know why he didn't sign it "love," but I figured he had come up against his admitted cowardice and had to pull back a bit. He had not mentioned his ex at all, a good sign. Anyone could see that he loved and needed Lily far more at the end of this letter than at the end of the one on which he'd scribbled the four-letters-and-a-comma that had made Lily's heart soar.

I turned off the dome light, started my car. It was early evening. Patty would be leaving for work soon. There was news on the radio; I switched it off. My headlights had come on automatically. I shut the car off, turned on the dome light, and reread the letter.

He wouldn't know what to do with himself if I weren't there to write to, he said. And then he opened up to me, if not the contents of his childhood, then better: the process of his thinking, as it was happening, at the edges of his comfort zone. I was getting closer to the fortress. I read the letter a third time.

Here I must admit a genuine if momentary admiration for Raven as a human being. What he did to CJ was disgusting, and Raven is a reprehensible and disgusting creature who should have been executed for the suffering he inflicted on the Stockings. But we are all bric-a-brac, odds and ends, as I have said twice before, and for a moment, in that parking lot, I wondered how life would have been if Raven had not decided to go to Diana's that night, had not shot CJ. Would he have been walking on a beach, working in a garden, fixing a fusebox, watching his children . . . ? Parts of him, behind the disgusting and reprehensible façade, were intelligent and ambitious and not immune to beauty. It was the nature of my mission to elicit those parts, corral them, prop them up, and then destroy them in as cruel a way possible. Sitting in my car in the Mailboxes Store parking lot that night, I wavered an instant, worried that I would not have the mettle to carry it out. To destroy the monster, I would have to destroy what was human in him, and what was human in him I could not help but admire.

I turned on the headlights, followed them home through traffic, considering on the way the various approaches I would take in drafting a response tomorrow, wondering how best to take advantage of this breakthrough, how to burrow my Lily-worm deeper into the dark and dusty chambers of his heart.

24

The lights were all on when I pulled up in front of our house—Patty was still at home. I pictured her peeking out the front curtains, waiting for me to return before she left for work, wondering why I hadn't gotten back yet. She had said more than once that the house didn't feel like a home without me in it, as if I were a coveted piece of furniture, or a pet.

I was in a good mood, though, and I knew she would chalk up the late arrival to my having had a good time with Calvin Senior. So it was with some surprise that I found her sitting on the living room couch, crying, surrounded by boxes and papers. If you've been paying any attention whatsoever, you can guess what those papers were, and you can do it in far less time than it took me.

I had walked in focused on Raven and Lily and tomorrow's work, and despite seeing Patty crying there on the couch, my attention was reluctant to leave those old thoughts behind, and I had to exert my will to focus completely on my wife, who shouldn't have been on the couch, shouldn't have been home, shouldn't have been crying. Only when I approached her and she scooted away from me did I look to the coffee table for clues to the source of her strange behavior. *Dear Lily*, I saw, *Dear Henry*. And the pages of CJ's journal I had xeroxed.

"Sweetheart," I said.

"Get away from me," Patty said. "No, I mean it. Go over there." She pointed to the other side of the room.

I tried an endearing look but her face did not soften. I walked over to the credenza and remained as calm as possible.

"Sweetheart," I repeated.

She winced at the word.

"My research . . . how did it get out here?"

"Research?" She sobbed. "Jesus, Owen, what are you up to? Where did you get these letters?"

"I can explain." Here I took a moment to collect my thoughts, wanting to give her a plausible explanation without spilling every last bean. I wanted to tell her just enough. When the end came, I would explain everything, and we would have a good laugh over this misunderstanding. "I'm sorry you had to see this stuff. It wasn't meant for you to see. Not yet, anyway."

"Not yet?" She held up some of the letters. "Please, Owen, explain this to me."

"Have you read the letters?"

"Will you explain where the hell you got this stuff?"

"Have you read the letters?"

She threw the handful of papers onto the table. "As much as I could read before I felt like throwing up. I've been going through this stuff all day, Owen. Is this really CJ's journal?"

"Yes."

She buried her head in her hands and moaned. I started to approach but she put her hand up to tell me to stay where I was. She had a way of controlling situations even when she had become completely unhinged.

"Did you say 'all day'?" I asked. "You haven't been sleeping?"

"We're not discussing that. Will you please explain this to me?"

"You sent me to the baseball game with your father so you could search my office?" She had to recognize that I was not the only guilty party here. Otherwise I was going to get nowhere, with her staking out the high ground. "You searched my office!"

"That is a separate issue."

"Is it?"

"Well, look what I found!"

"What if you weren't meant to see that?"

"Why are you hiding things from me?" I thought she was going to lose it again but she held herself together and stared me in the eye.

"I don't think it's right that you searched my office. However, I will explain everything to you on two conditions. First, remember that I love you and would never do anything to hurt you. Second, acknowledge that what you did—getting me out of the house and searching my office—was wrong."

"We're married, Owen. We're not supposed to hide things from each other."

"What about a surprise party?" I asked. "If you were planning a surprise party, you wouldn't want me to go through your drawers and spoil the fun, would you?"

She screamed in frustration, directly at me, then gathered herself. "If you would fucking explain yourself, we might get somewhere. I 'searched your office' because I was worried. You seem to be working too hard. You spend way too much time in there. I feel like we have no life together to speak of. I had to know what was going on. For the sake of us. I thought I might be able to help. That's why I 'searched your office'—and I didn't think I was doing anything wrong, and I still don't think I was doing anything wrong, because we're married, and you shouldn't be keeping things from me. Except maybe surprise parties, but this is not a surprise party. This is CJ's fucking journal. And letters from the man who killed him. And some woman. And it's creepy that you have this stuff—it's beyond creepy. I don't know what to do."

"Can I sit down?"

"Sit over there where you are."

"I can't come sit on the couch?"

"Not until you've explained yourself." I moved the rotating fan to the side and hopped up onto the credenza. Over the front window curtains, I could see someone standing in the parkway between the sidewalk and the street, waiting for their dog to finish his business, and then picking it up with a plastic bag turned inside out. How idyllic it looked to me, that scene under the streetlights. I would rather have been picking up dogshit with a plastic bag than sitting on the credenza, explaining myself to Patty.

Once she realized what I had done for her and her family, she would look past the shock of finding this stuff and appreciate my innovative and complex offering. I needed a little more time. Raven was nearly mine. I felt like one of those guys in the movies who barely has a grip on someone's hand as they're hanging off a bridge in gale-force winds.

"It's for a book," I said.

"What book?"

"I didn't want you to see it, obviously. It's research."

"You're using my brother and that scum-of-the-earth Henry Raven as research?"

"You see why I didn't want you to find this stuff. It's sensitive. I know. And I should have asked your permission beforehand, to write about him."

"You're writing a book about CJ? You're right, you should have asked me first. Take a minute to think, Owen. This is not just another story. This is my life."

"I know it's a cliché, but you have to write what you know. And—"

"A cliché? Did you hear me, Owen? This is my life. My my my. Not your life. Not yours to pick up and copy into a book."

It may not seem as though I was making much progress here, but in fact I was leaps and bounds ahead of the Owen who had walked into the room ten minutes earlier. We had gone from complete incomprehension and horror to a discussion over intellectual property.

"I didn't copy it," I said. "I'm not trying to steal your life. But if you're writing a book, you have to follow your gut and draw from the well of life. Otherwise you're wasting your time. My gut led me toward CJ. I had to know more. I had to do research. You were never meant to see it. You were only meant to read the finished product. I would have burned this stuff long before then."

"I didn't find any book."

"It's all in the computer."

"You didn't print it out?"

"It's in an encrypted file. I don't want anyone to see it until I'm done."

"You might have done a better job hiding your research."

"I'm sorry. I should have hidden it better, you're right. But I didn't think you were going to search my office. And I guess I saw it as already existing in the world. Not like the draft of the book. The draft has to stay in its womb a while longer. If it comes out too early it will not survive. That's why I didn't print it out."

"Can I see it now?"

"Only if you want to destroy everything I've worked on so far."

"How am I supposed to know whether I'm going to be comfortable with what you've written? I mean, Owen, this is really bothering me. How do I know you haven't picked us all apart in your book? What's to keep you from—even unintentionally—really stepping on people's feelings? Think of my mother."

"I'll let you read it first. If it bothers you too much I'll write a different book and never publish this one. I promise."

She remained guarded, but I could see her coming around. Her tears now weren't tears of rage or confusion but tears of semi-relief. It was all easily explained. Research for my book. Even if it was unorthodox or trampled on everyone's toes, it was for the greater good, for art. She could understand that.

"Let me get this straight," she said. "You stole CJ's journal."

"I borrowed it, copied it, and returned it," I said. "I felt horribly guilty about it for a while, then I began to figure that he would have wanted me to do it. He contributed in his own way."

"I'm still processing this, Owen. I don't know if I'm okay with that."

"I don't know if I'm okay with you searching my office."

"I was trying to help you out."

"I'm trying to help all of us out by writing a great book."

"What the hell is your book about, anyway? Why do you have to dig into CJ and his murderer and this woman who's obviously in love with him? What do these people have to do with your book?"

"You have to respect the process, Patty."

"I do respect the process." She blew her nose, then lay back on the couch. She spoke to the ceiling. "I just don't know what this stuff has to do with the process." I remained on the credenza. Cars drove by outside, birds chased each other through the trees. I have always been a synthesizer. At the end of an argument, I try to synthesize what has occurred. I can't help it. It's not a matter of having the last word, but more my way of storing the conclusions away in my brain. Patty knew this and was probably expecting my synthesis.

"I think we can agree that we have each trampled on each other's trust. I think we can agree that these events are going to take some time to process. I think we can agree that we are two people who love each other very much and do not want to hurt each other. Okay?"

"Yes." She was flat on her back on the sofa, her eyes closed. She said "yes" almost in a monotone. This was the voice of her rational self, overriding the swirl of emotion coursing through her veins.

"I think we can agree that the research materials you found were never meant for you to see, and that what really counts is the finished product. Can you be patient with me and wait for a draft?" I had to buy some time before I could drive the stake through Raven's heart, at which point I would explain to her exactly why I was doing what I was doing, and all prior confusion would become clear in that bright, retrospective light.

She sat up.

"Can I join you on the couch?" I asked.

She shrugged. I sat next to her. I put my arm around her. Her shoulders were tense. I pulled my arm away.

"I don't know, Owen. I don't know what to do with the fact that you stole CJ's journal from my parents' house. I know I searched your office, too, but that doesn't make either of us right."

"I'm sorry," I said.

"And why do you have letters—recent letters from the looks of it—between Henry Raven and this Lily woman? Where did you get them?"

"Research, I told you, it's all research."

"But where did you get them?"

"I have sources."

"Who? The prison?"

"I can't confirm or deny sources."

She let out a frustrated grunt. "It's bad enough you've got the letters of the man who fucking killed my brother, but the part that made me feel like puking, was how this desperate woman was glomming onto him like he was some catch, and all the while he's playing her."

"You think he's playing her?"

"He's giving her just enough to get what he wants. He's a sociopath, Owen. That's what sociopaths do."

"Sure he is, but he's got a heart, like anyone. She's got him wrapped around her finger."

"He's a monster, Owen. He doesn't have a heart."

"Maybe it's because you didn't read all the letters."

"I read enough. How she tries to dangle that teacher in front of him."

"Mr. Clancy."

"To make him jealous. And he doesn't even notice. Couldn't care less. He just wants more pictures and more of those porno letters. I don't know how anyone in their right mind could write so many disgusting sex letters to such a disgusting person."

"But the point of it is, she's playing him."

"What do you mean, 'the point of it'?"

"I can't explain everything or it will ruin the book. Be patient with me." I shuffled the papers together into a pile.

"No but you said 'the point of it,' as if you knew who had written all of those letters."

I didn't say anything in response. Her hands were shaking.

"You've been writing to the man who killed my brother?"

"You don't understand," I said. "Lily was created for a specific purpose."

She ran out of the room into the kitchen. I stayed on the sofa. I knew approaching her would be a mistake. I heard her take her keys from the key-hook. I was stunned. I could hear her moving aimlessly in the kitchen, mumbling "no, no, no" and crying. Finally, she sniffled loudly and went out the back door. I heard the garage open. I wasn't going to be able to stop her. Right now all she could see was a hundred strange pieces of a distasteful puzzle. I would wrap things up quickly with Raven. I had to remind myself how confident I'd felt before coming into the house. The shock of it all would blow over once I was able to explain what I had accomplished.

I went into the bedroom to lie down. The closet was open. Some of her clothes were missing. Where were the cats? I walked around the house, looking for the cats, but they were nowhere to be found. I checked the hall closet and their carriers were gone. She had been packed up to go even before I got home. The cats had been sitting in the car the whole time.

25

I awoke early the next morning after a fitful, alcohol-induced sleep. The sun burned bright and crisp—the weather refused to suit my mood. I made coffee and went immediately to my home office to begin work on Lily's next letter. The next few letters would prove crucial in cementing the bond between Lily and Raven. I understood that my strategy was risky, that someone else in my shoes might have chosen to go directly to Patty and apologize and beg and plead, thereby throwing countless months of work out the window. Think about the next letter to Raven: the line between success and failure would be as clear as the difference between a warm bed with wife and cats and a cold bed, or, as it turned out, a whole series of cold beds. A cold cot.

I worked day and night, making my way through draft after draft. I cannot even count the false starts and rambling explorations it took me to achieve the perfect tone and strategy. The pressure was almost unbearable. I did not answer the phone. I did not watch television or listen to the radio. I did not open the mail. I was an island unto myself. I ate what I could find in the house. I did not shave, I did not shower. I hardly slept, and when I did, it was on the reading chair in my office.

I dreamt Eileen was still alive and I had to explain to her, as we trudged inexplicably through a blizzard in parkas and cowboy boots, that I had used her pictures for a good cause and that she need not be afraid. Raven was not going to recognize her and think she was Lily and come after her. Eileen wouldn't listen to my reassurances. She warned me that Raven would indeed come for her, and that he would use her to find me. The dream faded on this warning as the waking world took over.

I included a Lily picture with this letter, an image unlike any of the prior ones. It was my favorite picture of Eileen, the one that made me feel I could have loved her my entire life had she not been my cousin. The set-up of the shot is unremarkable. She's sitting at a picnic table wearing a floppy hat, a bottle of mineral water in front of her. She smiles directly at the camera. If you look closely, you can see that there is some food on the table, half-wrapped in plastic and paper. An impromptu picnic. Way in the background, out of focus, is a cinderblock wall, and the middle ground is a grassy field. She had been in rehab for about a week when I went to visit her. She'd asked me not to take this picture, but when I did anyway, she smiled with such evident joy, with such optimism in her eyes, that I thought she might actually make it to a normal life someday. I had always seen in that photograph the Eileen who might have been. Might have been a positive young woman. Might have been a good friend to me. Might have been a doctor, a poet, a teacher's aide. A good wife to someone. I sent it to Raven unmodified.

Dear Henry,

You are the most courageous man I have ever known. And don't worry about what you would do with yourself if I wasn't here to write to. I will always be here for you, and you will always be there for me. If it takes time for you to open your heart, all the better for I will have known it was worth it.

Life has slowed down at school—Greta is back (her cancer is in remission) so I don't have to keep track of so much—and as a result I've got considerably more time to devote to our correspondence. I was thinking maybe I could even visit you sometime if your place allows that. I can't stop picturing it for some reason— the two of us, finally face-to-face, after all the intimate things we've shared already.

Late at night I lie here alone and I realize that you are the only thing in my life worth living for. I will let that stand even though I can't believe I wrote it.

I have enclosed a new picture. I hope you like it. It is my favorite picture of me. If you feel like looking into my eyes, go ahead. You will see there both promise and expectation. You will see the future, and it will be a long future. You will see the two of us, in the future. But it would be so much better if you could see me in person, and I could hear you speak, could see you smile. Mr. Raven, if it wasn't obvious to you before, I have fallen for you. The honesty of your last letter touched me in a way I have never been touched before. I haven't been drinking vodka and cranberry. I know you've fallen for me the same way. I just want you to tell me so. Tell me how you feel.

Very Truly Yours,

Lily

Every day I went to the Mailboxes Store and checked the box. I knew it was unlikely Raven would have received my letter, read it, and replied in such short order, but in situations like this, one hopes against hope. I did not want to miss his letter on the off chance things unfolded more rapidly than usual. More than once, I arrived before the postal service had delivered the mail, and so I found myself hanging around the Mailboxes Store, sometimes by myself, sometimes with other eager would-be recipients of mail.

On the seventh or eighth day after I posted the letter to Raven, it was just me and the man who ran the Mailboxes Store. His wife/sister was nowhere in evidence. (I wanted to ask him how his wife was, but I knew he would respond that she was his sister; if I asked him instead how his sister was, he would have told me she was his wife.)

My mailbox was empty. "Mail come yet?" I asked.

"Shouldn't be too long."

We stood around in silence for a while. I browsed the padded envelopes.

"Growing a beard, huh?" he asked.

"Why not?"

"Expecting anything good?"

"The usual."

He nodded.

A few minutes later, the mail truck arrived. A young female mailperson placed the mail in the PO boxes. Nothing. Another day of nothing. The man behind the counter saw me close the box without retrieving anything.

"Excuse me," he said, motioning me toward the counter.

I walked up. He frowned like he was going to say something unpleasant.

"I'm sorry to bother you, but . . ." He looked me squarely in the eye. "Is there someone I can call for you?"

"What are you talking about?"

"We're all okay and everything?"

"Are you asking me if I'm okay?"

He stepped back from the counter. "Forget it. It's none of my business."

"I guess not."

He laughed uncomfortably.

I went over this conversation in my head on the way home. I wasn't quite sure what had happened. He had tried to reach out to me. That much I could tell. But I wasn't quite sure what he wanted. Was it about his sister/wife? I wondered for a moment if I was dreaming. How could I know for sure that I was not dreaming?

In those cases when I have had a dream-within-a-dream-within-another-dream (the nightmare of facing mirrors and shifting time all rolled into one), I have always known I was truly awake when the resolution of detail suddenly increased. This is difficult to explain. Put simply, dreams seem real while you're in them, sure, but life feels, smells, looks, sounds, and tastes real.

When we're dreaming, all the stimuli are patched in directly. When we're awake, we have to filter out all kinds of insignificant stimuli in order to assemble a picture of reality. You can feel the filtering going on. My old test used to be: Can I taste the spit in my own mouth? If I could, it meant I was awake for sure. But the dream-mind caught up with this scheme. Weeks after I had devised the test, I had a dream in which I could taste the spit in my own mouth, but also in which I had sprouted wings and my penis hung to the floor, and I awoke from it in a state of great confusion.

26

I pulled the car to the curb. I reached into the glove compartment and retrieved the owner's manual. I found the index and looked for the fuses section. I scanned the fuse chart to make sure everything looked correct. Now I knew I was not dreaming. The fuse chart was there, and it presented itself to me in such exquisite detail, I could only have been awake.

I stopped at the coffee shop down the street before heading home. I needed a picker-upper. Everything seemed cloaked in gauze. So much of my sleep-deprived mind was focused on getting Raven's response, on waiting for the response, that whatever parts of it were not spinning in circles of worry were overtaxed, barely able to respond to people around me.

I hit a pole while pulling into the parking lot, putting a small but deep scrape in the front quarter panel of my car. I ordered a large black coffee to go and when I stepped up to the condiment bar to pour some milk in it, I noticed the Cartoon GI sitting at the adjacent table, with his four-color click pen, drawing conspiracy charts to post around the neighborhood. Cartoon GI grunted as he drew, spoke under his breath. I could only pick out one word of ten. "Fucking . . . multinational . . . torture chambers . . ." I took a peek at his drawings. NATO → U.K. + SOUTH AFRICA ← U.N. (ONE WORLD) and so on, with flag drawings in all four corners.

He looked up at me from under his helmet, then looked away quickly, focusing on the paper in front of him. I walked toward the back door. Buried in the series of grunts, I thought I heard him say "Purple purple panties."

Everything that went through the Cartoon GI's head came out of his mouth. His floodgates were always open, and a steady stream flowed out into the world. He held nothing back because he could hold nothing back. Everything came out, all the time. Talking about it is healthy. But nothing changes. We just keep on talking, talking, talking, until the end.

27

I had nothing to do for the next twenty-three hours, until the next mail drop. I went into the living room to pick up the mess I'd made of food wrappers and still-sticky plates and bowls. But I didn't pick anything up. Instead, I sat on the couch where Patty had sat before leaving me. I fell asleep and had a series of dreams in which the Cartoon GI was coming to get me.

When I awoke it was dark and someone was pounding on the door. At first I was convinced that it was the Cartoon GI, but as I reentered the world of the waking, I realized how unlikely that was. I looked through the peephole. Standing under the porch light was Calvin Stocking Senior, in his suit and tie, neck fat bulging over his collar, holding what appeared to be a pizza box and a six-pack of beer. I switched on the living room light and opened the door.

"Hey—holy smokes, Owen. You look like shit." Calvin Senior walked into the living room. "Your place looks like shit, too. I brought some pizza and beer. Thought we might talk. Unless now is not a good time?"

"It's fine. It's a fine time. Sorry about the mess." I bussed some dishes from the coffee table to make room for the pizza and beer. "I was taking a nap but I'm up now. Your timing's pretty good, actually, vis-à-vis my nap. Excuse me for a sec?"

"Sure," he said.

"Just going to put this stuff in the sink."

"No problem."

I dumped the dishes in the kitchen sink, ran some water over them. While the water was still running, I grabbed one of Patty's cookbooks off the shelf and scanned the index for something I didn't know how to make. Chicken Fricassee. I read the entire recipe to make sure I was indeed awake. . . . rosemary . . . ¼ teaspoon pepper . . . 3 tablespoons . . . add chicken parts . . . shake until well coated . . . combine remaining flour mixture . . . 30 to 35 minutes . . . 4 servings. . . .

"No need for that," Calvin Senior said. "I brought pizza." He had walked into the kitchen while I was reading the recipe.

"Sorry. I was checking something."

The sink had stopped up and was about to overflow. I shut off the water. A fly buzzed into the windowpane, looking for an exit.

"Let's go back out there," I said.

Calvin Senior grabbed a roll of paper towels and we returned to the living room. We cracked open two beers and started in on the pizza. I hadn't had hot food in days; the pizza was delicious. And the beer reminded me of our baseball outing.

"The reason I came, Owen, is that, well, you probably know Patty's been staying at our place this week." I nodded. "Now it's none of my business what's going on between you two—and I should mention that Patty doesn't know I'm here—but I wanted to see what I could do toward ameliorating your difficulties."

"I appreciate it."

"You understand that Patty is the most precious thing in the world to me."

"Yes, sir."

"And if you do anything to hurt her—I mean anything—I will have your balls in a sling so quick you won't know which way is up." He took a bite of his pizza and spoke with his mouth full. "But you're not that kind of guy, are you Owen?"

"No. I'm not. We had a misunderstanding. It's complicated."

"I don't want to hear details."

"It will resolve itself soon."

"No details."

"Okay."

"You see, I'm in a bit of a bind, here. I like you. But you've upset my daughter somehow. Emotionally I mean. So I wasn't sure if I should come here tonight. Then I thought, whatever it is it can't be worse than the shit I've pulled over the years. The kid needs some talking-to. Again, Patty doesn't know I'm here. And if push comes to shove, I'm on her team all the way. But assuming this is a regular episode of regular marital bullshit, I thought I'd hop the fence, so to speak, and see how you're doing."

"Thank you, Mr. Stocking."

"You're welcome. But frankly, you don't look good."

I wasn't sure what to say. "It's been a rough week. When Patty left, I sort of fell into a hole. Been trying to scratch my way out since. I don't know what to do with myself."

He looked pleased to hear me say this. "I've been there." He looked at my beer bottle, which was empty now, and finished his quickly. "Another?" We opened two more beers. We raised them and clinked bottles. "As I was saying, Owen, I've been there." He relished the opportunity to impart his wisdom. "It wasn't always sunshine and roses with Minnie and me. We had our ins and outs, too. She packed up and left on more than one night when we were first together. It's part of getting used to each other. Unless you've really fucked up."

"I don't know."

"Only time will tell."

"As long as she's patient enough—"

He shook his head. "Again, I don't want to hear it. If I hear it, I take sides, and I don't want to take sides right now. Things will work out or they won't. There's nothing I can do to help you on that front. But you've got to pull your shit together in the meanwhile. Be a man! If she decided to come back tonight, she would take one look at this living room and question her decision all over again. One look at you, even. Have another slice."

"I'm full, thanks."

"Then it's time for you to take a shower and shave. I'll clean up out here."

"You want me to shower and shave right now?"

"Damn straight."

"But I'm not going—I mean, I don't think things are going to sort themselves out tonight, between Patty and me."

"Of course not. These things take time. But in the meanwhile, kid, you've got to learn to take care of yourself, hold your chin up. I know. I've been where you are. Misunderstandings, whatever. I let myself go to shit. But I picked myself up off the floor before Minerva came back to me. You've got to have dignity. You've got to learn the habit of dignity. You walk around with your shirt untucked all the time. You're on the edge already. So when she takes off for her parents' house, you fall apart. No one ever taught you to be a man. Get in the shower and shave."

"Seriously?"

"I'll clean up out here."

I went into the bathroom and trimmed my beard with some clippers. I hadn't showered in days. I'd forgotten how good the hot water felt. I shaved with a blade in the shower. My skin felt slick and refreshed. Maybe Calvin Senior was right—maybe all I needed was to create my own sense of dignity. A shower and a shave seemed like a big step forward. I couldn't believe I'd let myself go like that. My father-in-law had always intimidated me, as the man who belongs to clubs, who knows sports, as Patty's protector. I don't know when his capacity for protection spilled over to include me, but I had never seen the scope of his emotional generosity before, and it amazed me. I grabbed a robe from the hook behind the door and went out into the living room. He had cleaned up all the trash and put away everything but the remaining beers. He was nowhere to be seen.

"Mr. Stocking?"

"In the bedroom." His voice came from the back of the house.

He had laid out my suit on the bed.

"When was the last time you wore that?"

"I don't know. I think we went to a wedding . . ."

"Put it on, you'll feel better." I put on the suit, including socks and dress shoes. Calvin Senior helped me tie a full Windsor. "There. You look sharp. Take a look at yourself."

I looked at myself in the mirror behind the bedroom door. I did look sharp. Much better than I had looked in the morning. And I felt better. I felt like accomplishing something. I could feel a distinct change in my attitude: rather than worrying Raven's letter would never come, I looked forward to its arrival.

We walked into the living room.

"Have a seat," he said. I did. He remained standing. "It's like wrestling an alligator, Owen. You're on top or you're on bottom. No in-between. Use everything you've got. I hope this thing between you and Patty blows over. And I hope you haven't done anything really stupid, because if you have, our next meeting won't be as kind." He shook my hand. "I have to go home to my family now. You should polish off those beers." He walked to the front door. "I was never here, okay?"

"Okay."

"Hope it works out," he said.

"Me too." He was out the door. Did I feel better, with my new dignity? Drinking beers in a suit? I don't know. When I'd finished the last two beers, I fell asleep on the couch.

28

I awoke late the next morning still in my suit. It was rumpled but better than what I had been wearing for the past few days. I went out and got myself breakfast at a local greasy spoon. People smiled at me as if I was going off to work, as if I was part of the team again. I ate my eggs with gusto and left a big tip. It felt good.

At the Mailboxes Store, the man behind the counter was relieved to see me "all cleaned up," as he put it. And I was relieved to find in my PO box, despite my getting there earlier than usual, an envelope from Henry Joseph Raven.

Dear Lily,

Do you know if this poet Percy Bysshe Shelley was ever in prison?

To——

One word is too often profaned
    For me to profane it;
One feeling too falsely disdain'd
    For thee to disdain it;
One hope is too like despair
    For prudence to smother;
And pity from thee more dear
    Than that from another.

I can give not what men call love:
    But wilt thou accept not
The worship the heart lifts above
    And the heavens reject not,
The desire of the moth for the star,
    Of the night for the morrow,
The devotion to something afar
    From the sphere of our sorrow?

                    Very Truly Yours
                          Henry

If Raven was indeed "not stupid," as he claimed, he must have known that the poem he'd copied would drive Lily mad. I can give not what men call love! The desire of the moth for the star! I admit I took solace in his "very truly yours," though the careful reader will note, as I did not, that the "very truly yours" was a verbatim echo of Lily's sign-off in the previous letter.

I cooped myself up in the house, scribbling draft after draft, looking for the right combination to melt his heart so that Lily's rejection of him—and how I dreamed of writing that letter!—would sting as much as possible. I was going to put a stop to it. I was going to shut Lily down, to return her to nothingness. I hadn't counted on my feeling her loss. Nor had I counted on my ineluctable empathy for Raven. Yes, I knew he was a murderer and that he deserved to suffer, but somehow in my plans I hadn't considered the coldness, the emotional fortitude that would be required of me to be the cause of someone else's misery like that. I had expected the justification to bolster me, but it wasn't enough. I had to harden my heart, do my duty, feelings be damned. My conscience would be clean, like an executioner's.

Dear Henry,

I was shocked by the brevity of your last letter! Having sent a picture, I expected at least a few pages from you. More than a poem. I long ago gave up on the idea of "what men call love." If you remember, that's what ended me up with a con man. I welcome your "devotion to something afar," but how about we shrink that distance down? I gave up all communication with Clancy and all other potential suitors to be with you, despite the fact that we can't be together physically! I am already in your heart now and I am real, Henry, and I can feel your soul through the pages of your letters, so the time has come to make things explicit, to un-cork your feelings and spill them out on the page. You would be lonely without me, Raven. You do not want to lose me now. Imagine your loneliness now and multiply it by a thousand. What would happen if I went away? Think about it. Tell me how much I mean to you. Imagine your life without me in it. Write to me and tell me how much it would hurt. You need me. I need you too Henry. You exist for me.

Lily

Maybe Raven would write back with a long declaration of love, maybe he would send another poem. Either way, Lily was close. She had penetrated Raven's pericardium . . . only a matter of centimeters to the dark center of his heart. Every day I visited the Mailboxes Store to check the box. It invigorated me to think that all my preparation was finally going to come to some frui-tion. No matter what Raven wrote in his next letter, I would stick it to him. Or maybe after two more letters from him. I kept up the routine of showering and shaving, kept dressing in my old suit. Calvin Senior had been right—it was possible to instill a sense of dignity in oneself by cleaning up and dressing right. I wondered how I could have ever lived otherwise.

So when Patty came to the front door one afternoon, after I had finished rinsing and drying my lunch plates, I thought I was finally going to cash in on my respectable exterior. I knew she expected to see what her father had seen. She was surprised to find me looking so clean and dapper without her help. It lent credibility to my plan.

She herself looked like she had had a rough couple of weeks. And yet she was a vision, all pale skin and large eyes. She'd been crying, which made her look all the more beautiful to me. Not for the fact of her having cried—this is difficult to explain—but for what crying did to her face: her eyes were bloodshot, the skin under her eyes was puffy and soft, and her lips looked fuller. One look at her, and all my emotional buttresses crumbled to the ground.

"Patty—I'm sorry about all of this. I miss you horribly."

Her eyes teared up. "I miss you too, Owen." She cleared her throat. "I decided to come over because I think we can try to put all of this behind us. We're married. That's something I take very seriously."

"Me, too. I know it's been hard. This was something I had to do."

"I don't think I'll ever understand."

I shook my head. "You'll be surprised. You have to be a little more patient. If you hadn't found the letters, you would have never known until the end."

"But this is the end, Owen."

"Almost, almost. We're very nearly there. It will only be a matter of days, and then I can explain everything."

"No," she said. "This is the end, Owen. Whatever you've been up to, it's over."

"Try to understand. I can't stop now. The finish line is a hundred feet away."

ANTOINE WILSON

She crossed her arms. "You don't know, do you?"

"What?"

"He's out."

"Who?"

"Henry Raven."

One part of me was total disbelief, the other plunging through empty space. I did my best to show no reaction, even as I felt the blood draining from my face, my stomach clenching.

"That can't be," I said. "I just got a letter. Lily just got a letter."

"He's out. Walked out yesterday. His conviction was overturned."

"How is that possible?"

"The bullet stuff got thrown out on appeal. Some moron judge ruled that the bullet-lead analysis tests weren't reliable. The DA doesn't even know if they've got enough to try him again. Owen, it's horrible."

"Yesterday. Where did he go? Does anyone know where he went?"

"It's over," she said.

I was very close to grilling her on the details—the bulk of my emotional momentum pushed me in that direction. But I knew I couldn't. I had to stop somewhere. I had to think of Patty. I sat at the kitchen table, head in my hands.

"It's over," I said.

"They fucking let him out." She shook her head. "How could they let him out?"

"They're idiots." I stood up. I collected myself. I stepped toward her, and she shied away.

"I think we should see somebody," she said. "I'm really confused, and I think we need to find somebody who can help us sort this out."

"Sure," I said. "Good idea." My voice was like someone else's voice.

"Why are you wearing a suit?"

"Just tell me when and where," I said. "We will work this out."

29

After she left, I dug through the stack of letters in my office until I found the one from Raven's cellmate, Moses Lundy. I immediately typed up the following note:

Dear Mr. Lundy,

I have been informed that Henry has been released. If this information is accurate, do you think you can tell me where he's going to be residing once he's out? He forgot to include a forwarding address in his last letter.

Sincerely,
Lily Hazelton

I tried to maintain as measured a tone as possible, in part to act as though it would be no big deal for Moses to provide

Lily with Raven's new address, and in part because it was the only way I could begin to calm myself. Was it true? Patty didn't seem to be bluffing, and had she been, it would have been too easy to catch her in that lie. It must have been true. Raven had never mentioned an appeal. Was it some sort of surprise to him? That wasn't how prisons were run. Raven must have been expecting it. He should have told Lily. I couldn't stand it. All of the emotional reticence I'd assembled for the letter to Moses Lundy started to crumble. I was overwhelmed by Lily's sadness, Lily's confusion. It wasn't fair. My head spun and my heart dragged. I was like a child trying to put a wooden block into a series of misshapen holes, not understanding that the block I held belonged to another toy altogether.

We had an appointment to see a couples specialist that Monday. I wasn't sure how I was going to approach the session. I didn't believe that anything less than the truth would be useful therapeutically, but I also didn't believe that telling the truth would be of much use to me. I still had to stick it to Raven somehow, and spilling the beans of my plan would not bring me closer to that goal.

I was in a therapy-pickle. Show up on Monday and go through the rigmarole about book research, or start to tell the truth and make some real progress with Patty. I was genuinely on the fence. Yes, I had a plan. Yes, it had been watertight and clever. But I was not blind to what was happening in my life and my marriage. I was not too stupid to know that the damage I'd done by now wasn't going to get magically stitched up. Tell the therapist the truth. It's the only way out. It is over. Then the feeling would return, the feeling in the pit of my gut the moment

Patty told me he'd gotten out, the primal feeling of anger I felt when I thought about how he had so coolly and cruelly dropped Lily without so much as a goodbye.

Could the man who had corresponded so openly and eloquently with my Lily Hazelton really be so purely cruel? Was all his tenderness and insight and soul-searching a simulation? I could not believe that. I knew Raven. Underneath the predator, behind the mask of cruelty and unfeeling, was a regular human being. How else could he have written Lily those letters? I did my best to keep that anger in check with the hope that Moses's response would explain everything.

Monday morning rolled around, still no response from Moses Lundy. I was supposed to meet Patty at the therapist's office at noon. I'd offered—in a gesture of goodwill—to pick her up, but she said the therapist preferred us to arrive separately for now. I guess the therapist didn't want us comparing notes on the drive home.

The only thing I knew about this session was that it was supposed to be a "fact-finding mission," each of us describing the series of events leading to our arrival at therapy. I still had not decided whether I was going to tell the truth. So much was uncertain. What if I were to spill the beans and then find that the overturned verdict thing had been an error, or that Raven was indeed out but he wanted to find Lily and surprise her in person? I couldn't tell the truth, not yet. But frankly I didn't feel like lying to Patty anymore. I had been very lonely lately and I wanted to patch things up. It is amazing how life can put us right on the edge of a sword. It might have turned out differently if we'd gone to the therapist in the same car.

30

I had some time to kill before the appointment with the therapist, so I drove over to Second City to check my mailbox. It was a windy day, and traffic was light. Trees waved their branches at me as I drove past, urging me toward my fate.

"Mail hasn't come in yet," said the wife/sister behind the counter.

I waited fifteen minutes, then left.

I was backing out of my parking spot when a postal truck pulled up. I reparked and went back in. It was about noon when I finally opened the mailbox. Inside was a letter from Moses Lundy. I unsealed it right there and read it. I was dizzy by the time I reached his signature.

"Sir? Are you okay?"

I needed to lean on something, so I leaned on the wall, but then I needed to sit, so I sat on the floor. Once seated, I needed to lie down, so I lay down, but even lying down, I still felt like I needed to lie down. . . . When I came to, the wife/sister was hovering over me. She had her hand on my wrist, taking my pulse. I had always found her to be strange looking, but now, with her face so close to mine and her clammy hand on my wrist, and me just having come to, she was a vision out of a nightmare.

I screamed. She leapt backward. The husband/brother behind the counter held his hands up as he crept toward the phone.

"Now, now," he said, "it's going to be all right."

"It's not!" I yelled. "It's not!" I snatched up the letter and ran out of the Mailboxes Store in a state of profound agitation. When I recollect that outburst—always in embarrassment—I picture the lonely mailbox key still stuck in its lock, its identical twin affixed to the same cheap wire ring, swinging back and forth in the turbulent wake of my departure.

Dear Lily Hazelton,

Henry Joe did get out, the lucky guy. He spent some time writing goodbye letters to his penpals but yours must have gotten lost in the shuffle. I know he's gone back to live with his woman in Mount Pleasant who has been keeping an eye on his truck and things since he went in. You can probably find her in the phone book, her name is Portia Snow, they been together a long time. Too bad you didn't get his goodbye note. Specially because out of all Raven's penpals we liked your letters best.

Sincerely,
Moses Lundy

I never made it to therapy. I went home. Straight to my computer, where I performed a directory search for Portia Snow in Mount Pleasant, CO. There was no Portia Snow listed there. No Henry Raven. I broadened the search to the whole state of Raven's incarceration. No Henry Raven, no Portia Snow. Finally, I generated a list of Snows, any first name.

P. Snow, Mount Pleasant, CO. A phone number. No address listed.

I threw the printout into my bag, along with a ratty, old, dying-battery laptop, the letters Raven and I had sent each other, the Xerox of CJ's journal, my microcassette recorder, and all the pictures I had of Lily and Raven. I ran into the bedroom and filled a suitcase with the most conveniently accessible clothing I could find. I would wear my suit no more.

It was only a matter of time before Patty would realize I wasn't going to show up. I knew she would come looking for me at home. I was in a rush. Nevertheless, I made a special, time-wasting trip to the front closet to retrieve our Frisbee, for what better memento of our time together could I carry with me out on the open road? I never used it, of course, for lack of someone to play with.

It was in the back of that closet, behind the rack of coats, below the shelf of board games, that we kept a safe. Among the items in that safe was a big wad of emergency cash. I opened the safe to retrieve it. Then, on impulse, I removed the Glock semi-automatic and ammunition, too. I was headed onto the open highway, with cash, and I would need protection from my fellow Americans.

I scanned the house quickly to make sure I hadn't forgotten anything. I stuffed some extra mouthwash and deodorant into my bag. I threw some food into a plastic garbage bag. I took a gallon of water from the earthquake kit in the garage. The car was loaded and I was ready to depart, but something was bothering me. I had to go back to my office. It held nothing I needed and yet I was forgetting something. The big desktop computer in the center of my work table looked like it was going to miss me, I thought, and then it struck me. The book. Patty would go looking in there for the book, and, encrypted or not, she would soon realize there was no book. I started up the computer, but it took a long time to boot up, and I was getting impatient. I had planned to copy some large document, encrypt it, and name it MY_BOOK.DOC or something like that. Instead I poured a half gallon of milk into the computer's tower, dousing the motherboard and hard drive with a gurgling, bubbling, creamy-white electrical storm.

The whole pileup was smoking when I ran out the door. I pulled out of our garage into our alley and drove to the end. When I reached the cross street, I stopped and looked in my rearview mirror. Why did Lot's wife turn into salt? Did I turn into salt when I saw Patty enter the alley, a block down, and drive into our garage, no doubt wondering what had happened to her husband?

31

I drove east. Out of Our Little Hamlet by the Sea, onto the freeway through the heart of the megalopolis, past the fiefdoms of the Inland Empire, and into the desert. A brief but powerful squall marked the end of the halcyon days. When the skies cleared they were not the same skies as before. Some force other than my will pulled my car forward, and that force would not be satisfied until I had found Portia Snow, and with her, Henry Joseph Raven. The fundamentals had not shifted. The scales of justice remained off-kilter. It was still up to me to balance them. I did not listen to the radio. I opened my windows periodically to make the rush of wind match what I was feeling. Desert dust rose from invisible trucks. Out there, everything had been stripped from the surface of the land, leaving behind only shadows. In those miserable sunny hours, my mind reeled with what I had left behind. A baffled therapist, a confused Patty, a clueless Calvin Senior, a sympathetic Minerva, a pair of keys, a PO box, a smoking computer, a collapsed plan. Their nagging pull was no match for the massive magnet of Mount Pleasant. They were gum on the sole of my shoe. At sundown I drove past blinking Las Vegas and considered for an instant where my life might lead if I decided to stop and gamble, drink too much, and then use the anxiety and guilt of my Viking Hangover to propel me, apologetically, into the arms of my sweetheart.

It would be another life, not mine.

At gas stations, at diners, on the verge of collapse, I brought myself back to life by reading the letters, by reading CJ's diary, until I knew it all by heart. All the wreckage was Raven's. He would pay. I had in my pocket, as the record will show, Moses Lundy's crumpled note. I did not reread it. I stuffed it away and forgot about it. His sentences were suffused with falsehood. I was under no illusions, however. Raven had, in a gesture of criminal camaraderie, shared some of Lily's letters with his cellmates. That I understood. I am quite sure he did not share all of them. And while he might have kept other second-tier penpals to occupy him while waiting for new letters from Lily, none of them had pierced his heart quite the way she did. It was impossible.

I made exactly two detours on that 1100-mile journey.

My first detour took me seventeen miles out of the way. 1.4% of my journey. Off the Silver Mine exit, up a two-lane road into the mountains. Pine trees, a clearing, a turnoff, and there it was, a low-slung, weathered wood roadhouse. Diana's Grill. I sat at the same bar, maybe on the same stool, as dead CJ.

Later in the night, I drove down a side road until I was in total darkness. I stopped and lay on the hood of my car, absorbing heat through my back even as the night air went to work freezing my features. The stars were breathtaking. Surely out there, among the stars, were other inhabited planets. Other intelligent creatures. Staring into their night skies. Alter-Owens, lying on the hoods of their little hovercrafts. All is not lost, I said to them, there is still time to set things right.

I fell asleep behind the wheel. I do not recall falling asleep, only waking up to the sound of my tires crossing into another lane. The driving threatened to sap my reserves. I decided that I would face him fresh-faced and clear-headed. Stopping at a motel was no indication of weakening resolve. I was strong. I was an arrow. But once I was in that mothball-smelling bed, sleep eluded me. I lay awake for hours, listening to the semis roll in and out of the truck stop adjacent to the motel, and to metronomic humping in the room next to mine. I clocked the woman's squeaks—the sound of a paper towel on glass just after the Windex has evaporated—at sixty-four per minute. The man was quiet. Finally I fell into a dreamless slumber.

32

At two forty-three the next afternoon, I arrived at the town of Mount Pleasant, a hillside community with a small, failing, alpine-themed ski operation. The entire place was covered with gray slush. No answer on P. Snow's phone. I scoured the commercial strip, asking questions at the local diner and the local pharmacy, but I came up with no leads. Those mountain people were naturally suspicious of strangers like myself. I could feel everything slipping away from me. It got dark. Things started to shut down. Still no answer on P. Snow's phone. I did not know where to turn next. Then, while driving around looking for a place to stay for the night, something familiar called out to me from a paint store parking lot.

Despite Brewster's Paints being closed, the lot, bathed in the orange glow of sodium lamps, was nearly full. Among the vehicles: a 1970s Dodge pickup truck. The color looked wrong at first, under those lamps, but when I pulled into the lot, the cross-eyed beams of my headlights revealed what I already knew.

This was Raven's truck, candy-apple red, the same truck I'd seen in that picture long ago. I parked a few spaces down and walked over to the truck, my footsteps crunching in the freezing slush. I could see my reflection in the paint. There I was, there was my image, reflected in Raven's truck. I placed my hands on the hood. It was still warm. Inside the cab, a red checked winter jacket lay across the passenger seat. The interior looked clean. I tried to tell myself that this could have been anyone's truck, that Dodge had made thousands of trucks just like it, that I hadn't actually tracked down my quarry.

Voices at the other end of the parking lot, some laughter. A pair of dark figures emerged from the alley behind the paint store, a short bearded man and a round woman, stumbling their way to a dilapidated car. They disappeared into the vehicle; it groaned under their weight. The engine turned over several times, weakening with every revolution. It started up finally, and I stepped through a cloud of blue smoke into the alley. There, tucked behind Brewster's Paints, lay the Hart's Head Bar. Two blacked-out windows, a rotting plywood door between them.

I pulled the door open. Smoke, stairs leading down. My eyes took a moment to adjust to the darkness inside. I descended, passed through another door at the base of the stairs, and entered the Hart's Head. People looked up, didn't recognize me, looked away. I leaned on the bar and ordered a beer. The room was lined with tall-backed booths; coats hung on the partitions, blocking the view into the booths. There was a jukebox at the end, and a pool table in the middle. Neither of the men playing pool was Raven. He was not on a bar stool, either. I would have to walk slowly through the place. I would have to pretend I was looking for someone. I was looking for someone. Classic rock emanated from the jukebox. The men on the stools were focused on some baseball game unfolding on the dusty television set above the bar. I asked the bartender for some change.

"To feed the jukebox," I explained.

I held my beer in one hand, but I couldn't figure out what to do with the other hand. The pool table's felt was covered with scars. Everyone was talking at once. I made my way to the jukebox. There was nowhere to put my beer. The song ended and everything was silent. I scanned the room but I couldn't see past all the coats. I went to set my beer in the booth next to the jukebox. A man was sitting there, alone. He looked up.

I had found Raven.

How many times had I considered what I would do with him when I found him? I had visualized pounding his face in with a hammer, kicking his lifeless body over and over, slicing him from gut to gullet. He looked at me with as blank a look as a man can make. I thought he'd recognize me somehow.

"Excuse me," I said, "can I set this here?"

He shrugged. I put my beer down. I fed the jukebox a dollar and hit random numbers until my credits were gone. He was only a few feet away. He'd cut his hair short, military-style. His chin showed several days' stubble. I should have destroyed Raven right then. I could have. Instead I returned to my beer. He sipped at his drink—whiskey, with a little glass of beer—and stared across the booth at nothing. The crack of a pool break. I turned my face toward the pool table, but my attention was still on him. I had to act as casual as possible while remaining vigilant. Distract the prey on the ground while the eagle dives from above. I should have picked up the ashtray and smashed it over his head.

Most of the booths in the bar were occupied. I turned to Raven. He did not look up this time. I could have walked away— every part of my animal self was telling me to walk away—but I knew I might never have this opportunity again. I had to steel myself. I cleared my throat.

"Mind if I join you?" I asked.

"Yeah," he said.

I sat down. The booth was smaller than I thought it was going to be, and the view different. The world was shut out on three sides, and partially obscured by hanging coats on the fourth. This was going to be an intimate showdown. Raven took a long drag off his cigarette. He exhaled slowly through his nose, flicked ash toward the ashtray. He had slender fingers, with little knots for joints. The jukebox played one of my random selections. Country, female, ballad.

"The jukebox busted?" I asked.

"How the fuck should I know?"

His eyes were on the pool game, but he wasn't watching it. He had been staring at the other side of the booth before I sat down, and now that I was in his way, he had to stare elsewhere.

"I'm just passing through," I said.

"Huh."

"I said, I'm just passing through town."

"I heard you."

"I'm from California. Out here to see a friend."

"California." He raised his whisky glass and drained it in one swallow. Then he polished off his beer. He started fishing around in his pockets, as if he might be about to leave.

"Let me get the next round," I said.

He lit another smoke, settled back into his seat. "Ten High, beer back," he said, not looking at me.

I left Raven sitting at the table. The jukebox played another song, more country. I ordered two Ten Highs with beer backs and brought them to our booth.

"I didn't pick this song," I said.

He sipped at his whiskey, made a face. "This Ten High?"

"That's what I ordered."

"Huh."

I would put him at ease. He would lower his defenses. He wouldn't know what hit him.

"I'm here to visit a friend," I said.

"In Mount Pleasant?"

"Cold Plains Correctional Facility. About a hundred miles east of here."

He shrugged noncommittally. But his eyes flashed. Try as he might, Raven could not conceal what was going on behind those eyes.

"You drive out here by yourself?" he asked.

"Sure," I said. "I'm alone."

One of the pool players walked up to the chalkboard next to the jukebox and crossed off someone's name. "Carl!" he shouted, "Carl's up!" Carl rose from a booth across the room, stick in hand, and proceeded to feed quarters into the pool table. Raven and I watched in silence.

He shook his pack of smokes. Nothing came out. He closed one eye and shook the pack again. Nothing. He started to go through his pockets. He rose from the booth and headed toward the bar. I watched him through a mirror above the jukebox. If he tried to leave, I would catch up with him before he could reach his truck and get away. I took a series of deep breaths. I was drawing him in all over again. He had left himself open to attack. I watched as he bought cigarettes from the bartender. He walked back toward our booth. He glanced in the mirror and our eyes met.

"It's funny," I said, after he'd sat down again, "you remind me of someone I used to know."

Silence. We drank and watched the pool game. Raven fiddled with the cellophane on his cigarettes.

"It's weird how much you look like him," I said.

"I'm not him."

"Because you sort of sound like him, too."

"It's not me."

"Good thing," I said. "He owes me."

"I don't owe you fuck-all."

"He owes me, is what I said."

"Exactly what does this guy owe you?"

"I'll know when I get it from him."

He smiled. I had amused him. I will forever remember that moment, when I had Raven in the palm of my hand. I should have destroyed him right then. I should have gone out to the car and fetched my Glock from the paper bag under the passenger seat, and I should have come back in and destroyed him, with the entire Hart's Head Bar as witness to justice finally, finally, served.

ANTOINE WILSON

But some invisible force held me back, told me to wait just
a little bit longer, to toy with my prey rather than dispatch the
monster immediately.

He shook the new smokes at me until one stuck out. I took
it. I did not want to deal with the consequences of not taking it.
I would have lost any advantage over him had I passed it up. He
took one for himself. He held out his lighter. I leaned toward
him, cigarette in my mouth. I could smell his breath. He lit the
lighter, cupped the flame. The tip of my cigarette danced around
in the little yellow flame. That moment, that instant in time, was
the closest I would ever get to Raven, physically. I was never much
of a smoker. I inhaled carefully. I did not cough. The first few
drags made me nauseous. The booze, the empty stomach, the
cigarette. We are undone by simple things. I had to grip the edge
of the table to stave off the spinning feeling.

"You make a habit of staring at people?" he asked.

"What?"

"If you're looking for the faggot bar, it's down another
block." Raven stood up. "I gotta take a leak."

After a moment, the spins dissipated. I let the cigarette burn
down, so it would look like I'd smoked it, then put it out in the
ashtray. I watched the pool players for ten minutes. Twenty.
Raven didn't return. Out in the parking lot, the red Dodge was
gone.

33

The empty parking space taunted me. Here was the poof of particles into thin air, it said, here was once the magician. You are the sucker. You and Lily are the suckers.

"Lily," I yelled, "Lily is the one who is supposed to disappear!"

"Shut up!" said a window on the street, and I wanted to go to that window and silence forever whoever had uttered that hateful phrase at me. I did not. I remained focused. The dragon slayer does not chase frogs. Or curse the sky, no matter how black and cold it may get.

Where is your resolve? I asked myself.

This is one minor setback, I told myself.

My car's trunk was full of resolve. I opened it there, under those color-shifting orange lights, those lights illuminating the empty space in which Raven's truck had sat. And Raven's tire tracks leading out of there, merging with and disappearing into the tracks of every red-blooded hillbilly who lived in that miserable gray town. I had my trunk open, thank god, or I would have spent the night in a fury hunting down random yellers in random windows and firing precious bullets at orange lights until the police showed up.

From the lid of that trunk hung one little life-saving countervailing tungsten bulb, shining on my files and papers (which they have taken away in an effort to unmoor me, I now realize, it was to unmoor me they did that) with the clement glow of soft white light. Soft white light! My world now is fluorescent. I am trapped in a green-lit box without my papers or files. But the trunk, what I saw in the trunk, if it didn't soothe me, at least it reminded me what was at stake.

I shed hot tears at the sight of CJ's journal, at the photographs Raven and I had sent each other, at the letters, the pile of letters, the documents, the tangible documents attesting to the briefest window of time during which two hearts had opened themselves to each other, despite all the odds, as they say. Of course it was a trap, and Lily was fictional, but who would know that, if they were to stumble upon our correspondence? Patty hadn't guessed it right away. I stood over the trunk in the cold night, flipping through pages, organizing my rage, focusing it. I had had a perfect opportunity and I had failed. I had succumbed to invisible forces. I would not succumb again. I could not allow myself to collapse into a tantrum. My mind turned involuntarily to the moment at which he had lit my cigarette, how I was so close to him. The pile of papers in the trunk. The gun under the seat. Raven somewhere out there. Owen.

What had Calvin Senior said? No one ever taught you to be a man. I'm teaching myself, I thought, I am following through on this, I am going to make it right again, I am not going to let invisible forces hold me back. I have never truly followed through, I thought, I have never had anything to follow through on, I have never been given the opportunity to follow through on anything.

I drove to an all-night gas station and convenience mart. I filled the car with gas and my stomach with coffee and pastries. Mount Pleasant was not such a big place. I would find him again. The factotum behind the register told me where the creeks were. The creek, the ravine, the green shed with white trim . . . I would find the world Raven had described in his letters, and I would find Raven again. His house was here somewhere, it had to be, and I would have my second chance.

I drove up and down those streets at just above a walking pace. A light snow had begun to fall. When I wasn't looking at every driveway, every little parking lot, every carport, I looked forward into a slow-motion undersea world, the result of which was that these roads and streets would unfold as long as I had the time and gasoline to drive them. Houses that looked like other houses went by one after another, the same parked cars again and again. I had driven onto some giant snowy Möbius strip. The screened-in porches floated past, as did the decrepit apartment buildings, the suburban-style homes. Fewer and fewer lights as I entered the early morning hours. My tires scraped the curb more than once as I tried to stay alert. There were police in that town, I know for a fact, but I don't know where they were that night.

I drove, I stalked, Mount Pleasant slept.

Who were these people, I wondered, and what were their lives? Did they know they had a murderer in their midst as they lay there, peacefully dreaming? I must admit I had to stop the car several times to wipe my eyes when I considered the contrast between these happy normal families and what had become of all of us, Stockings and Pattersons alike, as a result of Raven's actions. With one squeeze of the trigger, he had stripped us of the right to be all those other people, all those innocent sleeping people.

Some hours later, I refilled with coffee at the convenience mart. The factotum had been replaced by another, who wanted to chat. I was all business. I returned to my car to sip my coffee and watched, in the dank colonnade stretching across the front of the convenience mart, a lone black bird, feathers in poor shape, pecking around the back of an out-of-order ice freezer. There was a pay phone. I needed to hear her. I thought she'd be at work, and that I'd get to hear the voicemail greeting she'd recorded for us, back in the halcyon days.

She picked up on the second ring.

"Hello?"

Her voice was groggy. A moment before, she'd been one of the sleeping innocents.

"Owen, is this you?"

It was me, and it wasn't. I could not speak.

"Come home, Owen."

She breathed. She sighed. The line went dead.

At that moment, I built a wall within myself. I could not rest, I could not tear down that wall or even peek over it or drill a hole in it until I had settled accounts with Raven. Listening to Patty's voice, I had indulged a part of me I couldn't afford to indulge. I was swirling with invisible forces. There was no room for the sloppiness of feeling, for the way Patty and the sleeping innocents of Mount Pleasant had become involuntarily super-imposed through some hidden operation of my emotion-brain. In the movie version, a shadow-Owen remains at the phone as I turn back and proceed to the car, coffee in hand.

I took to the streets again, endless snowflakes spinning in the cone of my headlights, the same houses, the same lawns. The roads became slippery. I stayed my course. The sun threatened in its barely perceptible indigo way. I must have driven every street in Mount Pleasant. The things we seek are always in the last place we look. I know why it's so: because when we find them, we stop looking.

I found Raven's truck parked at the curb in front of a modest bungalow. I pulled up behind that hateful red Dodge, leaving enough room so as not to arouse suspicion. I tried to turn off my headlights, but they would not turn off with the engine running, and the engine was the only thing keeping me warm. I retrieved the fuse chart from the glovebox, not to see whether I was dreaming this time—I was not—but to locate the fuse for the headlights. It released from its socket with a snap. I idled there, in the warm darkness, the sun on its way up, and waited, focused on the door to that little house. I considered ringing the bell, pumping him full of bullets, but the man I had met in the Hart's Head seemed the type to answer the door with gun in hand. There would be no doorbell for Raven, just a surprise waiting for him at a point equidistant from his house and truck, a slightly familiar face, an arm, a hand, a gun. A few words. The end. I could wait all day. I had achieved a state. There was no doubt in me.

34

The sun rose. A fragile layer of white covered the mud and slush of gray Mount Pleasant. Birds sang to each other in the trees. The neighborhood sprang to life. Cars drove by. A burly man in a puffy blue jacket walked a pair of huskies down the street. I remained focused on the house, the door. Were Raven and Portia rising, dressing, making pancakes?

A yellow school bus struggled up the street, expelled a cloud of black smoke. I was reminded of something from my youth. When I was a child, I saw an advertisement in the back of a comic book for a series of punching dolls. They were pear-shaped vinyl inflatables, filled with sand at the bottom, and they would right themselves no matter how hard you hit them. Over and over again. One of them bore the image of an angry kangaroo, fitted with boxing gloves. Another was fashioned after an Asian martial arts expert, posed in a karate-chopping stance. But the one that struck me was the Penguin. He stood with his flipper-wings at his side, and his face was bright and open, with crossed eyes and a big smile. Even today, thinking about it brings me to the verge of tears. He was an image of pure, stupid innocence, and no matter how many times you punched him, he would pop back up, undaunted, ready for more abuse. I bought fifteen before I ran out of allowance money. I never blew them up, just stacked them, still in their original packaging, under my childhood bed.

My car windows frosted up. I wiped at the glass with a cloth, always keeping clear a porthole through which I could see the front door. The sky was brightening, the light was crisp, the house was still. I should state for the record that I was quite in my right mind at this point, calm and without fear. I had never felt more rational in my life, despite what those shysters tried to claim before I was forced to dismiss them and defend myself in a court of law.

I was calm and rational and staring at the front of the house when I saw movement across the street. I wiped at the side window. I saw Raven and Portia, not exiting the front door of the house I'd been watching, but exiting another house altogether, across the street. I had been staring at the wrong house.

By the time I hopped out of my idling car, they were almost to the sidewalk. The air had gone frigid without the insulating layer of clouds. For some reason the sun wasn't working very well. I proceeded toward Raven and Portia, annoyed that I had left behind my coat, that I would have to face them down while I was cold and they were comfortably dressed.

She was smaller than I had imagined her, and not as pretty.

They wore jackets and scarves, but their scarves weren't wrapped around their necks, and their jackets were unzipped.

I could see Raven's hat sticking out of his jacket pocket. They had just emerged from the womb of their home and were still warm with its heat. There was a cat in their front window, watching them go. This was my brain playing tricks on me, trying to get me to focus on the wrong thing. The cat would be well taken care of. I pictured Portia caring for it as she nursed her grief.

I walked quickly to intercept them. When I arrived at a point between them and the truck, I tried to stop too abruptly and lost my footing on the slushy road. I fell with a squish.

They were bearing down on me, now, and Portia wore a look of concern on her face. Raven smiled as if amused by my fall. I rose to my feet.

"You alright there?" Portia asked.

She was about to approach when she saw the gun in my hand. I raised the Glock. They froze at the edge of the lawn. Whenever I think of this moment, it is as if everything went into slow motion. Joe Dogwalker, on his return trip, had seen me lifting the weapon and was already on his way to tackle me from the side. And while I would have loved to give Raven a nice long speech before wiping him from the face of the earth, I simply pointed the gun directly at his face, some ten or twelve feet away, and pulled the trigger.

First there was the gun's report, then I was tackled to the ground by the blue-jacketed Dogwalker, who crushed me into the ice and snow of the street even as he wrested the gun from my hand. I let my face fall into the muck. It didn't feel cold at all.

I lay there on the ground, held down by Joe Dogwalker,

his putrid-breath huskies lapping at my face, until the police arrived. I bled from the nose. Pain bloomed in my shoulder and became more and more intense as I waited.

Sirens. This will probably come as no surprise, but when you shoot someone and are injured in the process, you typically have to wait for the second ambulance.

Not until I was lifted from the ground by a fresh-faced young cop did I see the first ambulance, into which they were loading an unconscious Portia Snow. What had happened to Raven? Nothing. He stood at the back doors of the ambulance, helping the medics load Portia inside.

How had I had missed him? I am no slouch with a pistol, and I had lined Raven up perfectly with the muzzle of the gun before pulling the trigger. If I had missed him, it must have been by a millimeter, I thought. And what about Portia? Had she fainted from fear?

I don't know how the physical world failed to heed my intentions that morning, or how a gun pointed at a man from a distance of ten or twelve feet could miss him so egregiously, or how—and this I did not discover until later, until I was in my own ambulance and the same fresh-faced officer of the peace was reading me my rights—the bullet which should have grazed Raven, if not penetrated his skull right between the eyes, ended up traveling through Portia Snow instead.

I am certain, beyond any shadow of a doubt, that the gun was pointed directly at Raven when I pulled the trigger. I am certain, too, that I heard the gun's report well before I felt any shove from the side.

My ambulance sped through town. We were driving down the wrong side of the road. I could see the police escort through the back window. I shut my eyes. The pain in my shoulder spiked with every bump in the road, every turn, every acceleration and deceleration. The police radio squawked. Paramedics. Portia Snow had died on the way to the hospital.

35

I share a cell with an older inmate named Clarence, who stabbed someone to death while robbing a car wash, of all things, in late 1997. He has been before the parole board more times than he cares to count, but they seem to have something against him. My only true companion, with gold-leaf cover and acid-free paper, is a book someone cruelly abandoned in the prison library: *The Greatest Love Poems of All Time.* I carry it everywhere I go, the pink satin bookmark at Walt Whitman's "To a Stranger."

I cannot help but return in my mind to the moment I pulled the trigger, to the gun's report, to the tackle. Raven had been right in front of me, staring confidently into the gun barrel, not surprised in the least that I was going to shoot him. She stood well off to the side. There was no way she could have jumped in front of him before I pulled the trigger. Physics took a vacation. There is no other explanation. I hadn't driven all those miles to shoot Portia Snow, despite what the cockamamie prosecutor had to say on the matter.

I'd imagined a victory speech at the end of my travails, a justice-was-done-one-way-or-another coda to cap off a blisteringly honest narrative of one man's search to bring balance to the scales of justice. I'd imagined, even as I knew things were getting difficult, presenting my story to Patty, helping her understand why I'd done what I'd done. The unveiling of a normal life. The lights were out, people crouched behind couches. But no one ever came into the room, no one yelled "Surprise!"

Patty and her family cut me off completely once it was clear that I was 100% guilty of the charges brought against me. My aunt and uncle, no great communicators in the best of times, stonewalled me. I resigned myself to living out the rest of my years with no one in my life. Institutionalization, meals, exercise, reading, keeping to myself. I would be a hermit in my own mind, a brain in a jar. Bounded in a nut, a king of infinite space. I'd seen them around the prison. Clarence had pointed them out. They were the shell-shocked, the dazed, the inmates who had broken out long ago, mentally, never to return. I would join their ranks, await the final reckoning.

Except that I am directly responsible for destroying a human life. I constantly bump my head against the fact that I can't turn back time and undo it. I suffer the most acute form of regret; my mind will not accept what has happened and can only think of trying to undo what I have done. I am all reverberations and shock waves. I look around the prison yard at other men, at those who are in for murder, and I wonder: You have eliminated someone from the planet. How does that knowledge not crush you every second of every day?

There is only one way to make it stop. Sleep, or its cousin. More than once I assembled a noose out of bedsheets. I strung up the noose, I put my head through it, but I could not make the leap off the bunk. At first, Clarence watched with amusement and curiosity. After a while, he dozed through my set-ups. I could not bear the cessation of consciousness, even if that consciousness was pure torture to experience. Each time I could not kill myself, the torture grew worse, because I had approached the boundary between life and death and had decided to turn back. I had pushed someone else over that line, but I myself could not cross it. My own death is a joke to me, but a joke I cannot bear to tell. Night after night. The physical facts of prison are nothing compared to what is going on inside my head.

I began this account eight weeks ago, believing then that only by writing my confessions could I save myself, restore balance again, cauterize all the old wounds. I offered up the only thing I had left, a few extra ghosts—may they persist in the memory. But there is no balance, the wounds bleed forever, I am not saved. The words keep coming, and nothing changes. You can talk until the front yard is flooded. All the talking in the world doesn't make a difference.

I still am haunted by that look of Raven's, by the confidence of his glare, and by the glint of recognition that lay behind it, as if he knew why I had come, knew that I would not succeed. How I wanted to watch his body crumple to the ground as I filled it with bullets! I could have lived with that, extracting from him in reverse the pain he'd inflicted on Calvin Junior, on the Stockings, on Lily Hazelton. All the damage, compressed into dense pellets of lead, backed up with gunpowder, finally coming home to roost, all over Raven's body.

But he escaped the fate I had so carefully constructed for him.

I would have shed exactly one tear for the author of those letters as I pumped him full of bullets, and that would have been that. Instead I killed Portia, somehow, and the still-living Raven of my mind cannot shake off the speck of humanity I've stuck to him.

It is the noblest mistake to see humanity in everyone.

Fifty-six days have passed. Shard of a life. Every morning when I awaken in my cell, I picture Patty, over a thousand miles away. She's pulling closed the bedroom curtains, darkening our room, crawling under the covers for another day of sleep. I see the glass of water at her bedside, the water evaporating. There's no one there to refill it.

We get two hours a day outside for exercise. Yesterday I found myself at the edge of the yard, standing by the first row of chain-link fencing, with an unobstructed view. They set this place down on the plains, a hundred miles from anywhere. On the blue-gray horizon, I saw the faintest outline of those majestic mountains to the west, the mountains separating me from all I have known and loved, the mountains in which the Stockings lost their CJ, the mountains in which Raven now roams free. I stood close to the fence, the wind stinging my eyes. The peaks began to change shape. The mountains drifted across the horizon. Clouds. A buzzer sounded. It was time to go back inside.